Titles by *L*

T0146768

Doctor Frederick Ngenito

Linus T. Asong

Langaa Research & Publishing CIG
Mankon, Bamenda

Publisher:
Langaa RPCIG
Langaa Research & Publishing Common Initiative Group
P.O. Box 902 Mankon
Bamenda
North West Region
Cameroon
Langaagrp@gmail.com
www.langaa-rpcig.net

Distributed outside N. America by African Books
Collective
orders@africanbookscollective.com
www.africanbookscollective.com

Distributed in N. America by Michigan State
University Press
msupress@msu.edu
www.msupress.msu.edu

ISBN: 9956-616-14-1

DISCLAIMER

The names, characters, places and incidents in this book are either the product of the author's imagination or are used fictitiously. Accordingly, any resemblance to actual persons, living or dead, events, or locales is entirely one of incredible coincidence.

Contents

Dedication

Dr. Wefuan Jonah and his Entire Medical Crew Who Took such Great Care of Me during my prolonged illness at the Bamenda General Hospital. It was During This Time That the Story Took Root in My Mind.

Part One

Chapter One

His patience wearing desperately thin and, regretting the fact that his good friend Raymond had not been available to drop him in his personal car, Fred said: "Taxi man, I beg, hurry up," for perhaps the fifth time. He knew the interview was scheduled for ten, so he left at nine, knowing that whatever happened he would be there in forty-five minutes. But after forty-five minutes he was still a kilometre away. The taxi man stopped after every few yards to drop off or pick up another passenger. At one point Fred urged him:

"Massa, I beg, just go straight, I get some very important meeting for attend. I dong even late."

The man didn't look bothered. A woman who sat directly in front of him struggled to turn and look at the man who was urging a taxi driver to leave his passengers and go straight, but the effort failed her. She was very fat and huge and had even been taken because she had accepted to pay twice the fare, which was a hundred francs. She was very black, with a small head that grew from a huge neckless body. Her back as she sat squeezed in the small seat

But, although she did not succeed in looking at Fred, she had made her point: the gesture suggested that she condemned anybody telling the driver what to do. Fred would discover that the fat woman's negative reaction to his comment was meant to pre-empt any other comments that would arise as a result of the fact that she would take them far out of their way. They had to leave the main road and drive over two hundred yards through the quarters of bumps and pools of stinking water with ducks flapping their feathers and splashing muddy water all over the place. At every junction when they stopped the driver enquired: "This one?" she responded, pointing a thick, short and round finger: "No, de ora wan."

Finally, all the passengers were furious and began shouting deprecations at the driver who himself got angry and stopped and ordered her to descend. She was not of the size that could be pushed out, she could only be persuaded. Luckily she did not protest, although she was speaking furiously to herself. Apparently the taxi had come to stop very near her house because as she rolled away three naked children with dripping nostrils and swollen bellies rushed to meet her, chanting, "Mammy élé, ya ya yo!"

"Why you no be lefam I drive enter fo ya parlour put yu for dey?" the driver shouted to the woman as she banged the door angrily.

The woman was not to be outdone:

"Yu tink say we de pick that money na fo pick'am? Thief ting."

"Michelene Tire, timber weight, goods only," the driver spat out breathlessly as he reversed the car and they drove back towards the main road.

After that comment Fred noticed the futility of pushing the driver any further, who wove in and out of the streets and byroads until he saw that he was the only one left. Even if he wanted to, he could not get down because he would not find another taxi coming that way for a long time. He felt trapped and nervously he glanced at his watch every second. About two hundred metres from town towards the scene of the interview the road took a downward plunge, such that he could see the entire building from that distance. There was only one black car in the front yard, and a few people loitering in the veranda, probably the other candidates, or some workers, probably both. "African time," he told himself with a mixture of relief and condemnation.

Relief that after all that waste of time, he had not been as late as he had feared; and condemnation because he personally made a fetish of respecting time.

"Here, my man," he told the driver when they arrived the entrance above which stood the signboard: K-TOWN PROVINCIAL MINISTRY OF HEALTH. From squeezing himself in between the two other passengers Fred noticed that his *Terelyne* suit was slightly crumpled and dusty. With his brief case held firmly in his left hand he took out a sparkling white handkerchief from his pocket and dusted the knees of the trousers which showed, more than any other part, traces of dust. Then he stamped his feet several times to shake off whatever dust might have settled there.

Clasping the bag between his thighs he pulled at the bottom of the coat downwards to straighten it. Then, releasing the bag and holding it in his right hand he straightened the pair of trousers as he passed through the iron gate and started climbing the steps leading to the front yard of the old building, scaring the colourful lizards that lined the steps, nodding endlessly as if to welcome him. For a fleeting instance he thought of Puss, his father's black cat which would have had much to rejoice at if it showed up at the steps. His father kept cats not because they were likeable pets but because they rid the compound of rats. When there were no rats, or when they went into hiding as they quite often did, Puss went after the lizards. It single-handedly eliminated lizards from a compound the size of two football fields. Puss was not actually a name as such. It was the way a child of the family called the first cat that was brought to the house. Thereafter, every other cat was called Puss. Even when the cats littered and the house was full of them, everybody called each of them "Puss."

You mounted the thirteen dirty steps into a front yard that would have been more appropriate for any other institution than a Provincial Ministry of Health. It was bestrewn with dry leaves which kept falling even as he stood looking at the tall and old mango, pear and eucalyptus trees that provided a shade round the compound. To the right stood the most eloquent evidence of a once powerful presence of the Germans, a broken bust of OTTO VON BISMARCK, "the iron chancellor," with his heavy bald head and thick moustache over a small mouth and descending into both sides of a receding chin, his left breast covered with medals of honour of meritorious services rendered to the German people during his lifetime.

In front of the fallen bust was a fountain that gave up water in jets which sprayed into a circular pool of dirty greenish water beneath which lay dead frogs, broken bottles, empty milk cans, rags, scraps of zinc. Viewed from the air, the building itself, an ancient German Courtyard, had the shape of a small letter "n" with offices occupying its two sides while the top was a gigantic hall reserved for conferences, voting during elections, weddings, dances and any other ceremonies. It turned out that the interview was to take place in the big hall.

A veranda ran right round the entire building with cement pillars supporting the roof on all sides. Outside, on either side of the building lay in gigantic heaps, the carcasses, chassis, wheel drums, tires and shattered windscreens of antiquated vehicles; here an AUSTIN OF ENGLAND, there a M*A*N DIESEL, LANDROVER, RENO, HOOVER, LADA, BEDFORD etc. The bodies of most of the carcasses had been carved out by tinkers to make shovels, hoes, cutlasses and other household items and farm implements. If he thought the Ministry of Health was untidy, he ought to visit the Provincial Ministry of Health...

To the extreme right of the veranda, as you climbed the three or four steps that led into the main building, and leaning on the ledge, were some three gentlemen, all very well dressed, conversing in soft tones. Fred concluded that they must be candidates for the great office. Walking up to them he bowed with a brief respectful bow, greeted and introduced himself: "Frederick Ngenito Mutare, M.D. Edinbra." He made sure his medals were visible as he greeted them and he expected that if they were cultured people one of them would make reference to them. To his discomfiture, nobody looked at them.

Chapter Two

The three men introduced themselves too: the tallest amongst them who was nearest Fred spoke first. Wearing a simple but very well-embroidered *jumpa*, a blue traditional necklace and a cream pair of trousers that matched the *jumpa*, called himself Joshua Ening. On his head was a very large and pointed traditional cap which added to his height. There was colourful embroidery in front, by the sides and behind the cap. He did not mention his title. He wore a very broad smile that showed a gap in the front teeth. He conversed throughout with his hands clasped behind his back and seemed to swing from side to side as he spoke. He was fair in complexion and there was in his small Mongolian eyes a genial look. He spoke clearly and he had the habit of adding "of course" to everything that he said. He was clean-shaven, had high cheekbones and pointed chin.

The second man, of medium size with quick darting eyes and nimble fingers spoke with an affected American accent which did not succeed in concealing his Franco-phone background. He introduced himself as Dr. Philip Matanglia. He was wearing a charcoal grey suit. The sleeves of the coat almost covered his fingers, such that you wouldn't know he was wearing a shirt inside unless he stretched his hands, which he did ever so often. His head was slightly bald, his forehead lined but well oiled, and his eyebrows thick over the glittering eyes. His lower lips looked reddish or bruised and he bit it whenever he was not speaking as though he was conscious of it and did not want people to see it. His neck was thin, such that there was a large gap between his shirt and his rather pronounced Adam's apple which left his broad tie hanging loosely.

The third man, slightly taller than Matanglia, but not as tall as Ening introduced himself Dr. Bruce. He too was slightly bald but his hair grew thickly on the rest of his very light body. He had wide pronounced eyes behind heavy-rimmed goggles and kept twitching his right eye as if something had dropped in it, but it was a habit. He kept a heavy beard which he pulled at from time to time and spoke in a deep sonorous voice. His fingers were long, so too were his fingernails, and with the layer of long black hair covering them, one was oddly reminded of the hands of a chimpanzee.

Of the four, however, Fred looked the best dressed, and if the dressing counted, he would have received the highest scores. His dark brown suit fitted his great height like a glove. He wore sparkling brown shoes and carried a brown brief case to match, which everybody noticed at once. Inside the coat was a petty coat which held the tie in place. On his left chest were two medals: the first bore the image of a bird sitting on an anchor. Below were the words "Dr. Musgrave Memorial Medal of Honour." The medal was annually awarded to the best student in the field of surgery in the Faculty of Medicine. The second was a chalice held high in the air by several needy hands and with a stethoscope hanging from it. Below it were the words "University of Edinburgh Faculty of Medicine Medal of Honour." It was awarded to the best student in the field of private research. Fred earned that in his research on tropical medicine, specifically, in the area of Malaria and Tuberculosis. Both medals were of gold and glittered proudly, invitingly against the deep brown background of his suit. They all conversed with great cordiality although each saw in the other a threat to his acquisition of the great office and so spoke rather tensely.

Suddenly two cars arrived, a black Mercedes and a white Peugeot 404. Everybody recognised the pot-bellied, ugly-looking gentleman who emerged from the Mercedes as Honourable Sam Edimo, Member of Parliament for Likenge, Kumba Central. He was dressed in a deep blue *agbada* with sleeves trimmed at the shoulders, exposing his white singlette, his bloated stomach and folded sides. He was smoking a big long, curved pipe which gave off chunks of smoke and an offensive odour. He was certainly one of the judges, and he emphasised this point by passing into the building without caring to greet anybody.

From the other car emerged a man and a woman, both of the same average height. The lady was described as Lady Sussan Fonocho, Chief of Service of Administration and Financial Affairs at the Ministry of Health. She was the representative of the Minister of Healthy for the occasion. Although she was an architect by upbringing it was not surprising that she represented the Minister whose highest qualification was a B.Sc. in Physics and he was the principal of a high school at the moment he had been appointed Minister.

Lady Fonocho wore a light blue skirt under a light blue coat, a light blue hat on a black wig of hair that reached down her shoulders, light blue shoes and a light blue handbag. On each of her wrists were three golden chains. Inside the coat was a sparkling white lace material. On her left frontage of the coat she wore a brooch which carried the image of two little birds on the branch of a tree. A thin woman with large breast and thin legs on unusually high-heeled shoes she stilted her way into the building, straightened her dress, looked left and right and walked in, across to the conference hall. The gentleman who came with her was the obnoxious Mepako Lazarus, who occupied the obnoxious office of Government Delegate for the K-Town Council, a congenital idiot. It was a strange office invented and superimposed on the people of Kumba who unanimously voted against the Government during the Council Elections, in order to undercut the force of the opposition. A man of very little education, he used the office to humiliate all those who voted against him, and secondly, to build up a private fortune for himself, which he did with absolute impunity. He was a detested man who got the office by virtue of the fact that his father was once a mayor of Kumba.

The fourth person to arrive was the Director of the Provincial Hospital, the very popular Dr. Aloysius Ngale, a dark bespectacled middle-aged muscular gentleman with a feminine face and voice. He spoke shyly but confidently. He was a renowned surgeon who could hold his own against the best anywhere. He was holding a small leather file jacket, and was wearing a black suit made of very light material which trembled furiously in the gentle breeze that blew. He was known to be very devoted to his job and was very much loved by both his workers and patients. He was the only one amongst the judges who took time to greet the candidates.

Last to arrive and, appropriately so, was Alhadji Danpulo Sariki, the Governor of the South West Province. Having been several times to Mecca, there was an oriental look about his dress: he was wearing a three-piece yellow-to-white *agbada* elaborately and daintily embroidered round the neck, hands and legs. On his large head was a high cap with just as much beauty and embroidery as his *agbada*. The sky was a hard blue without a single cloud in it and the sun had not yet started shining brightly. This subdued atmosphere added splendour to the richness of the man's clothing by toning down the whiteness which would otherwise have looked too strong and rather offensive to the eyes. He was of average height and with a skull that had the shape of an inverted pear, did not look intelligent at all. He was dark in complexion, clean-shaven and spoke with a broad smile.

He looked perfectly harmless and spoke English too perfectly for a Northerner, but the people of the South West held him in very great disfavour. It was common knowledge that he had done nothing during his seven years stay at the head of Government in the South West that could be said to have made the place better than he found it. On the other hand, he had milked the Province dry, using prisoners and material destined for construction work in the Province to build villas in his village in the North. He is said to have usurped the role of the Commander of Public Security and was engaged in unravelling plots against the state, crushing plots and protests. He was carrying a black walking stick and walked with a dignity which befitted his position as the Chief Executive of the Province. A Gendarme Orderly walked close behind him, bearing his brief case.

From the look of things, Fred concluded that this was not going to be an academic exercise like the gruelling interviews back in his university days in Edinburgh which he still remembered with a grim shudder. The interview which was supposed to take place at ten eventually opened at eleven forty-five. No explanation was given for the delay, and no apologies were rendered; it was as if everything was being done strictly as scheduled. The right end had been carved out of the very large hall for the interview. The walls were draped in green. A large oval table of polished mahogany stood at the centre with five chairs on one side on which sat the judges, and one on the opposite side for the candidates. In front of each judge stood a bottle of mineral water; there was another one for the candidates. A messenger stood by ready to serve the water at the crack of the fingers.

When they were all seated, Lady Fonocho came out and announced the order in which they were to be interviewed: Dr. Bruce Minkanta, Dr. Joshua Ening, Dr. Philip Matanglia and finally Dr. Frederick Ngenito Mutare. The interviews which Fred described later as a parody of a medical interview, lasted exactly one hour and, each time a candidate left the hall he simply walked away without even waving to the others, a behaviour which made the others more and more nervous. When it was Fred's turn he walked in, greeted and sat down. Lady Sussan Fonocho who seemed to chair the event introduced herself briefly to him and then asked:

"Dr. Ngenito Mutare, what do you think the duties of the Director of Medical Services for the South West entail, even without having been one before?"

Fred was brief and to the point: "I would presume that it entails co-ordinating the activities of the various medical institutions of the South West Province, noting their problems and reporting back to the Government with possible proposals for the solutions."

"Thank you, Dr. Ngenito Mutare," she said and turned to Honourable Sam Edimo who cleared his throat and asked:

"Dr. Ngenito Mutare, there I have received letters from my militants who have noted with very great disappointment, the gradual turning away of patients from the Government hospitals in favour of private clinics and the like. If you were made the Provincial Director of Medical Services, what steps would you take to recapture these lost grounds?"

Fred sat up and reflected for a while before saying: "There are ever so many reasons why the patients prefer the private clinics, the least of them being that they are cheaper. On the contrary, private clinics are the most expensive. Patients go there or are taken there rather than the Government hospitals because, I guess, there they are promptly attended to. I say "guess" because I am new and do not quite know what obtains. Secondly, I would implement a move whereby medical services rendered to civil servants are charged to their salaries rather than demanded on the spot when they or members of their families are ill."

There were silent nods of appreciation. The Director of the Provincial Hospital went close to clapping. He whispered something to Lady Sussan who sat next to him and sat back, folding his hands.

"Finally, I want to guess again that the nurses in the Government hospitals may be too rude to patients. If this is the case, then I would institute a system whereby the patients before they leave the hospital rate the behaviour of the nurses and doctors who attended to them during the period of their stay there. I would then hold periodic meetings with the staff at which the ratings of the patients would be discussed. In conclusion, I would summon the staff with the lowest ratings and talk to them individually, while offering a gift to those with the highest ratings each month."

"Satisfied," Honourable Sam Edimo said and then turned to Mpako Lazarus, the Government Delegate.

"Dr. Ngenito Mutare, when you go round the hospitals, you find broken hospital equipment, microscopes, stoves, beds, and the like. I know how often the Director of the hospital has approached me for assistance to have those things repaired or replaced. We have written to the government and waited forever. If you were made the Director of Medical Services for the South West Province, how would you take care of this problem?"

"Maintenance culture is dismally lacking," Fred said even before the man finished talking. "You cannot stop a microscope, a bed or a stove from getting bad. But getting bad is not the end of its life. These things do not die like our patients do...."

The Governor chuckled and the Director of the Provincial Hospital held down his head and smiled to himself. Fred continued:

"They should and can be repaired. We have young men and women from the technical colleges looking for jobs. We simply set up a repair shop for hospital equipment. We advertise positions with expertise in maintenance of hospital equipment such as microscopes and even x-ray machines. We also make it open to the public and we use proceeds from jobs done to the public to pay them. They will work miracles. That's the way I see it. Even while that is going on, I, Frederick Ngenito Mutare, have international connections. I have in my home right now thirty-two microscopes and packets of reagents which were donated to me free. If I were made Director of Medical Services, I would simply enlarge my contacts and before long all our problems would be behind us."

"Satisfied," Mpako Aloysius said. When Lady Fonocho looked round and discovered that nobody was anxious to question the candidate any further, she told him:

"Dr. Ngenito Mutare, you can leave us. We will keep in touch."

Fred thanked them and with a respectful bow left the room. At the threshold, the Governor who had not asked him a single question called him back and reminded him, looking at Lady Sussan Fonocho for approval, that there would be a second interview of all the candidates in a fortnight. Lady Sussan Fonocho smiled and thanked the Governor for reminding them. Then he enquired about Fred's marital status. He told them he was not quite married but that it was up to him to decide when to get married. He told them that he had a fiancée to whom he could get married.

"The point is that we have not yet gone to court mainly because I had not thought it urgent…"

"It is now urgent," the Governor said. "The office of Provincial Director of Medical Services has never been held by a bachelor. On Saturday, 27th October, in this same room at the same time, this same Commission will meet finally on this issue. If you can decide with your fiancée, get duly signed legal documents to indicate your changed status, it will do us both a lot of good."

"I will be married."

"We will be glad."

16

Chapter Three

Down the road as Fred walked, expecting a taxi, he laughed at the parody of an interview of the Director of Medical Services. Nobody had asked him where he studied, although it could be argued that that could be got in the CV he submitted; nobody asked him about his field of specialisation and how that skill could be applied for the betterment of his people. They spoke as though the major killer diseases, malaria, typhoid, yellow fever, T.B and the most recently HIV/AIDS pandemic that were ravaging the entire continent were a figment of the imagination, problems that belonged to an entirely different planet. He had come ready to explain the measures he would take to curb the spread of HIV/AIDS, the researches he had begun abroad to destroy the malaria gem, the contacts he had made to treat typhoid and T.B. Nobody had given him the chance to show his usefulness to the country. Instead they had concentrated on banalities. It was impossible to believe! As an afterthought, he reflected on the composition of the jury and recalled with a touch of sarcasm what his old headmaster, the snuff-taking, diminutive Osi Kemakem used to say about dull or careless parents who blamed their children for poor academic performances or persistent misconduct: "You cannot make silk from sow's hair."

Nobody seemed to notice the two hard-earned medals which he kept brandishing to everybody's view. Nobody asked him to describe the nature of his intellectual attainments, even briefly. He wondered whether the other candidates had been asked similar questions, more difficult ones or easier ones. He would not be surprised if one of them said he was asked to sing the National Anthem, recite the alphabet or something as ridiculous as that. At any rate, the interview did not impress him. He did not know how Raymond would receive it. It may sound quite ordinary to him.

But one thing struck him though, and he took note of it as something to discuss with Raymond as soon as he got home, the fact that they insisted on him getting married. This pointed to one thing – they thought him good enough for the job so he did not want to be faced by any extenuating circumstances. The thought crossed his mind whether he had acted prudently in saying he had a fiancée. He did not have a fiancée, he had girl friends. But they were as good as fiancées. He forgot about the taxi and continued walking until he came to a roadside bar where he called for a cold beer.

As was the practice in the vicinity of all Government offices in the country, there were several bars down the road from the main block of the Provincial Service of the Ministry of Health. He went into the one with the rather attractive name of GARDEN OF EDEN. There was a touch of irony in the choice of name: the surroundings did not reflect the name, there were no flowers to remind one of the biblical Garden of Eden, no chairs, only benches and tables that were supported with pieces of wood to prevent them from collapsing. Fred asked the boy serving to clean one of the benches for him, which he promptly did and then even without asking him what he would drink began to play his music so loud that Fred could hear nothing else and it took him a lot of calling for him to come back and take his order. The small house was made of sun dried bricks with the inside of the bar and the entire front so carefully plastered and whitewashed that you would think it was a cement block building. The owner seemed to take an interest in sports: there were almanacs of great football teams of the past, Uruguay, Brazil, Argentina, Germany, and Italy. On another wall there was a picture of Mohamet Ali and Joe Frazier, one of Mohamet ali and George Foreman and yet another of Mohamet Ali standing over and rebuking a fallen Soony Liston, daring him to stand up and fight. There were also a pack of musicians: Mariam Makeba, Jimmy Cliff, Jim Reeves, Michael Jackson, Elvis Priestly, Ray Charles and Stevie Wonder.

He begged the boy to lower the music and then he began to drink, reviewing the activities of the day, taking casual stock of and assessing the girls he had encountered ever since he returned to the country. He did not allow his mind to wander too far afield, however, although he could not count how many girls he had met and spoken to.

One week after he returned to the country, Raymond Mbongli, his primary and secondary school pal who now headed an Agricultural Extension Centre at Barombi Kang, got together with some friends and organised a cocktail party at the Community Centre to welcome him back home.

To help recover some of the expenses incurred for the party, as Raymond later explained to him, the party ended up in a grand gala dance to which the cream of the town was invited. The gate fee was a flat five thousand francs. He was introduced as the guest of honour and, when the moment came for the opening of the floor he was one of six gentlemen paired with six ladies to do it. The partner with whom he was paired was an enigmatic lady. As the M.C put it, "our guest of honour, Dr. Frederick Ngenito will dig it out with no other person than our glamorous queen, the most talked about, the charming beauty, Miss Beatrice Affeseh."

A live orchestra, usually a great and rare attraction, was on display, backed by several local DJ's. The M.C. was Raymond himself, and the number he chose for the opening, a choice which was influenced by Fred, was a Highlife number, LOVEM ADUREY, by the late Rex Lawson of Nigeria. The opening of the floor lasted just one minute before the music was lowered to permit the M.C. to ask everybody else to join, before picking up again. When the music was lowered, some of those who opened the floor resumed their seats. Fred loved dancing, but, out of courtesy he was just about to lead the Beatrice lady to her seat when he noticed that she had seized his right hand and turned him round to continue dancing back to the floor. They joined the rest and continued dancing. Fred recalled that the girl danced that and any other record very well. Fred too was a good dancer and at a certain moment their performance drew a long applause from the crowd. Fred recalled that she monopolised him and made it look as if the two of them had come together to the dance. Fred recalled that he danced with very few other girls. During the dance she had introduced herself to him and they had had occasion to talk very intimately.

Fred recalled that after the dance he asked his friend Raymond why he had paired him with Beatrice for the opening of the floor. "That girl can suck the hell out of you," he added.

"I thought we should try something," his friend had confided. "That girl always proves tough and extremely reserved. I personally gave her the invitation. I thought she would refuse."

"Tough!" Fred said to himself. How could she be described as tough when she could crawl like ants on a complete stranger? He could not recall how many times they kissed on the floor when the lights were dim. He recalled how she sent her tongue so far into his ears that he feared she would burst his eardrum. That was not his idea of toughness. But, to give credit where it was due, she was beautiful, not only at first sight, not only that night, but ever thereafter. Fred visited her several times afterwards and they even went out for drinks. But he was wary of the girl that had fallen, as he put it, at first shake. That was a metaphor from harvesting mangoes. Sometimes some mangoes still hanging on the trees were so ripe that they fell just as you stepped on the branch. Some, although ripe, would resist any degree of shaking, allowing unripe ones which nobody wanted to fall to the ground, to the annoyance of the harvesters. But he kept up the relationship all the same. This was the lady he was thinking of when he assured the commission that he had a fiancée. There was nothing to be ashamed of about her as a wife. He would go straight to her and break the good news, and after that drive down to Barombi Kang and acquaint Raymond of the way things had gone.

Very many years ago, perhaps fifty, perhaps more, the whole of the area now occupied by the Down Town Government Primary School was the staff quarters of the CDC workers whose rubber plantations covered hundreds of acres of Kumba land. There were two types of houses, the wooden houses for the labourers and the brick buildings for the intermediate staff which numbered about two hundred. People whose relatives lived in those camps in those days retained sad memories of the conditions under which they lived. Whole families with grown up daughters and sons were jammed into a single room. Parents made children in full view of the other children behind curtains as transparent as mosquito nets. One toilet served ten houses and woe betide anybody who had the urge to go to the toilet when the line of people waiting was long. Inevitably, human wastes littered the camp, especially the gutters. But the white men who owned the plantations were never bothered by the filth and unhealthy conditions. They were only interested in the attendance of the people at work. Besides, the workers did not feel cheated at all. Instead, they enjoyed camp life and painted life in the camp in rainbow colours whenever they wrote to their friends back home, especially in the North West Province. The result was that more and more people flocked to the C.D.C plantations, despite the deplorable conditions under which they lived.

As the town grew and the plantation receded farther and farther into the countryside, the wooden houses and some of the brick buildings were pulled down. Now only twenty-one of them remained for the teachers of the school.

Beatrice lived alone in one of these little houses, two small bedrooms and an equally small sitting room. Each room had a small window, the parlour had one small window also and two doors, one leading to the back and the other to the front. The back door of Beatrice's house opened to the main road. She kept it permanently locked but opened the window which was also to the back as often as necessary.

Chapter Four

K-Town is a big city, one of the biggest in the country. But in a strangely important sense, it is a small place. People know each other and it doesn't take long for people to know that there was a stranger around. This is especially common amongst the intelligentsia. Civil servants make up an insignificant fraction of the entire population. The rest are farmers, small, medium size and big businessmen. And as a natural concomitant, it is also a city of crime. Money-doublers, *faymen*, sorcerers, prostitutes of the worst kind, and even outright robbers, all made K-Town a haven. Talking of prostitutes, one of the streets was oddly named CONFIDENCE STREET. It originated from the fact that it was the first part of the town to be inhabited by prostitutes. If you failed finding a woman anywhere else in town, you were "confident" of going home with one if only you made your way to that quarter.

You could count by the fingers of one hand children who grew up with Frederick and made it to the top in academics. They were once very many, but with the passage of the years a good number died, through natural and non-natural causes. Thus every grown up girl in college knew the number of Kumba boys who were in the universities abroad and when they would or might be returning home. One such person whose movements were very closely followed and very well known was Frederick Mutare. Opinion seems to be unanimous on a good number of points concerning him. He was brilliant, he was unmarried, rich, intelligent, self-respecting, respectful though proud and even supercilious.

Many people were glad that he did not marry a white girl which was very much the fashion at the time for young doctors. It is said that his father had warned him against it and he had promised not to disobey him. He was the topic of conversation amongst ladies who were still unmarried. Many condemned his womanising tendencies very vehemently in the open but secretly wished they featured on his list of women to be used. They all wanted a piece of him. They said he was very choosy, very hard to please, miserly and the like. Many condemned him openly but went to pray secretly that God should deliver him into their hands as a husband.

One person who listened with keenest interest at what was being said about Frederick before they met and even long afterwards was the same Beatrice Afesseh whom Fred was going to visit. Much of what they praised or condemned in him pleased her very much – superciliousness, self-respect, choosiness, austere, fastidious tastes, his very reserved nature. And many of the comments they made about him were similar to those that were made about her. In particular, they condemned her tendency to shun men or even treat them with obvious contempt, of not behaving the way other girls did, to behave as though she was above everybody else. Perhaps her strict religious upbringing had to do with it, but Beatrice was in her own small way, a breed apart. They also wondered, sometimes to her hearing, what kind of man she would get married to.

Amongst her friends she was considered too careful, too proud, too demanding in terms of natural qualities she would like to see in people. She had this cruel tendency to look low on men in general. She had a very poor impression about men. She believed that it was difficult to love a Kumba man because he comes to you with the purpose of conquest. He gives you the impression that you are his all. Once he succeeds in going to bed with you, his mission is ended.

The next thing he does is that he moves over to your best friend and gives money and continues to go round, leaving behind a trail of hurt feelings. She usually said that what God had given women which men want so much is too precious to trifle with. It is to be protected jealously and not to be gambled with. She would reprimand her friends for their frivolity and promiscuity:

"The fact that we are not married does not mean that we should sell ourselves at so low a price."

"You never can tell," one of his friends would say. "You have to try everybody because you do not know where your luck will come from."

"The way you are doing it, the way you are going about it, by the time the man who really wants you comes up, there will be nothing left in you."

It will always be there, sea never dry " the friend would say. "There is always enough to go round."

Beatrice was unmarried and whenever Frederick's name was mentioned, she would keep discreetly quiet. In her mind she prayed that he should remain unmarried by the time he arrived Kumba and she would make herself familiar to him. She had never actually met Frederick but what she heard about him pleased her so much.

Being an immensely creative individual, the whole scene in which he broke the news to her rose in Fred's mind's eye like a film on a giant movie screen with him striding across that world like a colossus. He saw himself at her house, sitting with Beatrice in an arm chair, the kind they called "me and my wife." He was sipping a drink. When he felt that he had rested enough he announced his intention of getting married to her. She was extremely happy, especially as she would be the wife of a Director. Who wouldn't? There would be so many cars at her disposal. The advantages are numerous. She completed the scene by pointing out that:

"From the day you asked me for a dance, I knew that something bound you and me and that some day that something will manifest itself."

"It pays to be patient," he told her in his reverie.

Very deep in thought, the taxi he had taken arrived his destination, Beatrice's house, without his noticing it. He came back to himself just in time to ask the driver to stop. It was Saturday and he knew that if she went to the market she must have returned home by then.

She was really at home. Returning from the market, she had changed from her wrapper outfit into a multicoloured *kaba* which was freer and more loose on her. She had been sitting in her small parlour, glad to be home after a hectic two hours in the market, having to put up with all sorts of people: the small girl crying because someone had stepped on her wounded toe, the lady bending down to pick up an ear ring and then finding that she had lost her purse in the process, the man selling fish, trying to outdo the second hand clothes dealer in shouting, young boys selling sweets or biscuits, the old man shouting and holding up a string on which he had pinned packets of needles, rolls of plaiting thread, small combs; then there were the pigs, howling as if they were going to be slaughtered, fowls, ducks; the man selling medicines for teeth, or was it teeth he was selling? The boy selling ladies' pants which he advertised as though they were table covers or some flask: "cover for massa yi chop! Buy cover for massa yi die!" Everything was on sale. It was a madhouse, and she was lucky to have escaped without losing a shoe.

When she heard a car drive up and halt down in the street she opened the back window and peeped. She did not look as excited as she would have been, or as she once was when she noticed that it was Frederick. But she smiled all the same and went to the door where she waited until he had climbed down, paid the fare and then climbed into her

26

veranda. She thought Frederick a kind of tempter, a handsome tempter who could raise a lady high and dry. The kind of person a lady of respect should handle with very great care because he was far too insensitive to the feelings of others towards him. Or he was completely incapable of discovering the feeling of others towards him, especially of those who loved him dearly. For all his great learning, he seemed incapable of judging character, she thought. She had once loved this gentleman with all her soul, and she had done everything within the bounds of imaginative possibility to show him, to make him see or at least guess that she loved him. But he had taken too much for granted and had refused to see it, or had ignored it. That had hurt her like a dagger through her heart. It had hurt her in a way she did not think Fred would ever make up for. She came to see in him a firm warning to be more careful with men in future, an embodiment of the mistake she had made and one she shouldn't make again. In any case, life must go on.

"Freddy, welcome," she greeted first, offering him her hand which he seized and for the first time detained for more than a few seconds after answering her greetings. But for his unpredictable conduct, he was such a charming gentleman, very irresistible. Just the kind of man a lady would be proud to keep company with.

"I see you here once in a blue moon," she said quite frankly, a comment which should have put Fred on the alert and compelled him to straighten that out first.

"Come on, Betty, don't say such a thing," Frederick said, throwing her hand off as if the accusation offended him. "That your blue moon must certainly be less than a week," he said.

"Even one week is a very long time," she said softly.

There was a silence during which he looked round the house with a renewed interest that she had never perceived before. Then he said very intimately:

"Absence makes the heart grow fonder. The son of Man shall come at a time when you least expect him, it is written. What have you brought for your dear from the market?"

There he goes again, she thought, raising her hopes only to dash them to pieces. "I have no dear," she said, smiling but with an undercurrent of seriousness which Frederick did not fail to catch. Then she asked with some interest:

"Who is my dear?"

Frederick did not answer, he simply smiled back and rephrased his question:

"What have you brought for me from the market?"

She looked at him for some time and then asked: "so you are my dear-eh, Freddy?"

"Am I not?" He was not looking at it as the joke she took it all to be. She did not know that this time he was talking in earnest. She uttered a short sharp laugh and there was a sudden silence which she broke with:

"That's really good news for me. I have brought oranges only. I would have brought something nicer if I knew that *my dear* was going to be here." There was an ironic emphasis on "my dear."

"How could you not expect me on a week end like this," Frederick pressed on, preparing the ground to land.

"There have been several weekends in the past," she said softly.

The accusation was point-blank. He knew she was speaking the truth and this made him remain silent with guilt. She took out three oranges, washed them, washed her hands and started peeling them silently. Frederick made such a great impression on her, long before they ever met at the ball. And immediately following the party, she thought he really the kind of man she could fall deeply in love with. Gradually she regretted the fact that that interest was waning. Yet, she could not resist the urge to serve him. She could not tell him to leave her alone, that he was blocking her chances with other men. When she had peeled the oranges she took out a very beautiful saucer from the cupboard and placed the oranges on it before serving him.

He took one, she too took one. While they were sucking the oranges she called for a small boy and sent for drinks.

"Gold Harp for me."

"I know," she said, and sent for an Export for herself, the most popular drink of the time. Before the beer came she had set the table with the most beautiful glasses that she possessed. When the drinks were brought she opened them, filled Frederick's glass which she handed to him and then drew a side stool and placed in front of him. They began to drink. She offered him all those nice services just to let him see what he had missed through his own carelessness or presumptuousness. Because of his dubious attitude towards her she no longer looked on him as the God that she once thought him to be. He was just an ordinary man endowed with some great qualities that could be well used, but which he had opted to abuse. Not a man on whom one should invest her emotional capital.

Frederick's thoughts were different. Having made up his mind to love and to hold Beatrice for better or for worse, she had suddenly or gradually begun to appear more glamorous, beautiful, a lot more beautiful than she had ever been. She may not be the most beautiful girl in town, but she was not bad for his purpose. There was not much to be ashamed of in having her as a wife. She would be made to look more beautiful as soon as she tastes comfort.

"Come and sit by me here," he said striking the cushion to his right on the large *me and my girl* armchair exactly as he had seen in his fancy.

She smiled to herself and came up and sat by him, mechanically, as disinterestedly as if she were play-acting.

"Come nearer, very near me," he said. She shoved nearer him. He asked her to serve him another glass of beer which she did. Then striking an attitude of seriousness he said:

"Betty, I would like us to have an important talk sometime later today."

"An important what?"

"An important talk."

"When?"

"Later in the day."

Her lips drew taut. As a result of what she interpreted as his coldness towards her, Beatrice had long decided that she would not allow anything that Frederick did or did not do to disturb her. It would not shock her if he came up one day and declared that he didn't want to be with her anymore. The way she saw it, their friendship, if we could call it that, had ceased to have any serious meaning. But when he made that pronouncement, she looked afraid and embarrassed but without knowing why. She swallowed loudly and remained silent. Frederick couldn't fathom her thoughts. All he noticed was that her breath had quickened suddenly like that of somebody in the grip of a fever. After a reasonable pause during which she tried in vain to master her surprise and amazement she asked:

"Why only later in the day?"

"You have just returned from the market, you need to eat and rest first."

"You want me to rest and yet you are at the same time making it impossible for me to want to rest..."

"How?"

"By withholding the secret or whatever it is." What kind of important talk could it be that he wanted her to eat and rest first before listening to it?"

"Is it bad news?"

"It is no bad news. It is good news, very good news."

Then give it to me before I lose interest in it."

"I give you a hint. What is it that girls need most?"

"A dress?"

"Try again."

30

"A baby?"

"No."

"A house of their own?"

"You are getting closer," he said. She was sitting to his right and at the time he announced the intended *important talk* his right hand was clasping her left hand firmly. Now he tightened his grip further before releasing it gradually and then putting the hand over her neck until it rested on her right shoulder. Lowering his voice to a conspiratorial whisper he said the magic word: "Marriage!!!" and then followed with "I am suggesting that we get engaged for marriage. We have known each other long enough and so before our familiarity breeds any contempt we should take that major decision on our relationship.

A silence fell. He could feel a sudden pumping of blood in the artery of her left wrist which he was holding over his right thigh. Or was it his own blood that was pumping? He could not immediately summon his medical practice to interpret the symptom. He had spoken like a deity announcing to an ordinary mortal that he had been given a place in heaven. And why not? Was he not a deity in his own right as far as women were concerned? He had the ultimate weapon, the supreme seductive powers against which few women have ever had any defences. Now that circumstances had compelled him to bestow the favour – what else can he call it – of taking a lady as life partner, no other girl deserved that favour better. She had that charm, that particular glow of well being for which Frederick would want to fetch her out.

Chapter Five

Her reaction had been completely worked out in his mind's eye: as sure as death, as sure as morning follows night, she would, or better still, should, cannot help but, jump up and dance about and throw herself round his neck and kiss him until his lips turned red for making her dreams come true. But the reality seemed different, very much different, quite the opposite of the dream.

Beatrice did not jump up in excitement. She shifted a bit away from Frederick so that she could take a look at his entire right side. The expression on her face was elusive, an admixture of surprise, shock and anger. Her mind pulsated so hard and fast that only a series of deep breaths restored her equilibrium.

"You get what I mean, Beatrice?"

The silence deepened. Did he stammer? Did he punctuate his words with audible gasps? Or did those sounds come from somewhere deep inside his mind? Unlikely. Not the kind to be nervous, worse still, to show nervousness – to a woman. Quite unlike him.

Beatrice did not answer. She bent slightly forward so that Frederick's right hand slipped from over her neck to the middle of her back. She supported her head in her right hand over her right knee. Frederick threw a careless glance, looking for a clue on her face as to how she was taking the proposal. His muscular left hand had long unclasped her left wrist on its own accord and lay across his stomach. He repeated the question, his voice taking on a drawl that under different circumstances would have been described as truly comical.

Her lips pursed and curled with sullenness and disinterest, an unfinished scornful smile froze on them.

"I do," she responded at last but carelessly.

"And what do you say?"

That silence again, worse than all the din in this world. There was something portentous in the ceremony which preceded her answer, whatever it was going to be. She seemed to lean forward more and more on her elbow which ground into her fleshy thigh as if to give her words maximum weight. Her expression was calculated to leave no doubt that she was not about to express joy. Frederick was an expert at body language and read that fast.

"You said you were only suggesting, not so, Dr. Frederick?"

Dr. Frederick? His right hand which he had thrown behind her back and round her neck and was pecking at strands of hair on her right chin, now rolled completely off her back as if gently caressing her back and fell onto the cushion. A spider-like shiver raced up his spine. She shifted even farther away and straightened up as if she had been virtually imprisoned by the heavy muscular and hairy arm over her neck. He lifted his glass towards his mouth and then returned it to the side stool without tasting it. When he lifted his glass he noticed that his hand trembled a bit, an indication that he was getting very nervous at all that was unfolding. He turned and looked at her. She was staring directly into his eyes, worse still, she must have noticed the nervousness he was trying to conceal. Frederick! He repeated to himself. It is true that it was his name, but Beatrice never called him that. She called him *Fred* or *Freddy*, or if she wanted to be a bit formal she said "doc." Only his parents and his teachers called him *Frederick*. No girl ever called him Frederick. So when she called him that way it did not sound like his name. Or if it did, it was as though somebody were insulting him. It seemed to suddenly place him miles away from her. And this was the moment he needed to be closest to her.

A sardonic smile visited his dry lips. His eyes now widened with an implacable gaze moved slowly, assessingly across her face. He warned himself not to entertain any fears, to think of nothing short of total success. He bore too strong a record to panic. He was born handsome and before he was fifteen he had had two sexual encounters with adult women twice his age – having been seduced by the women. The first of these ladies became Miss Cameroon the very next year. In Europe he had wooed and won and gone to bed with French, English, Spanish, Dutch, American and Chinese girls, and girls from places he could scarcely recall. In all these conquests he had never repeated his request before winning the lady. In several cases it was the women who wooed him. To win a war in Europe and lose in your backyard, was like surviving a storm at sea only to drown in a tea pot. That was not speaking well of him. In all previous cases involving women, he had been in need of a pint of milk only. Now he wanted the whole cow, a different ball game altogether. The main thing was that he was preparing for a job, not the moment to grapple with disgusting alternatives. Anything different from a "Yes" would be more than a humiliation. It would be a catastrophe because it involved his honour, not so much the job...

"Frederick," she interrupted his ruminations, "let me suggest something too."

"Do, Beatrice." The nervousness had now come to the fore, it was unconcealable, and had fastened itself on his voice which now vibrated like a poorly strung guitar string.

"Give me time to think it over because I have not been thinking of you along those lines."

Frederick smacked his dry lips and used his tongue to wet them. He glanced at his watch and let his trunk lean back comfortably in the chair, closing his eyes slowly. The discussion had worn him out tremendously and he actually felt like taking a nap. There was so much silence that a mouse dashed across the floor from the kitchen and then dashed back into the room. Beatrice saw the tricky mouse and had thought of getting up and shutting the door of the room and trapping it and killing it in the parlour. But her mind was too disturbed by the topic under discussion. The silence persisted and you could hear Frederick's watch ticking away his luck, his unbending pride and self-confidence.

Frederick had actually gone to sleep, during which his fancy again set to work and he saw himself in front of the anxious commission, brandishing a marriage certificate. He saw himself being congratulated by his other contestants as well as members of the commission. Then something caused him to open his eyes. Exactly six minutes had passed during which he had travelled through space and time. He glanced at his watch and then asked;

"Have you?"

"So that was the time you were giving me like that, Fred? I thought you were just resting your brain."

'You asked for time to think."

Her lips came firmly together and then she barked a long derisive laugh and rose and went and sat by the dining table which stood in front of them, a few metres away.

"That's too short, Fred. Give me a long time. Days, weeks, months even."

"It shouldn't take you days to make up your mind, Beatrice."

"It should take any girl who is serious about it months, even years, to make up her mind about you, Fred. You need to be studied like a book. You need to be chewed swallowed and digested before being understood."

She allowed the silence that had set in to run its course. Then, with a memory for injuries that brought Frederick to the edge of the armchair, she enquired;

"Fred, did I not ask you from the very beginning where our friendship was going to end?"

"You did," he answered with self-conscious candour.

"You remember what you told me, not so?"

Why should she retain all this? He thought he remembered, but he didn't. He chose to remain silent. When she asked again he said:

"I am not sure I remember."

"I don't blame you. The only reason you do not remember is because you do not particularly care about the effect of your conduct on others. I still remember what you said. Very well. You said 'time will tell.'"

His lips pulled apart in a long grimace. She continued:

"I asked you whether I should make our friendship known to my friends or relatives or both. You said I should not run faster than my shadow, by which I took it that you had refused. So the relationship was to remain at the level of a shadow. I have since remained with my shadow. After that you never said anything about the relationship until now. I was with you last week, I know the meeting was as brief as usual, but it was long enough for an important talk to have been discussed. Nothing. You continued to be as cold as ever. I find it hard to understand what has prompted you to come and propose marriage today and demand an answer immediately, when you have never done anything to make me imagine even remotely that you love me to the extent of making a proposal and demanding an immediate answer.

"That weekend following the party there was going to be a dance at the Customary Court Hall. I came to ask you if we should attend, something it would have been your place to ask me, if you were not just tempting me with your request of friendship. You said at first that you were not feeling well. When I stayed longer, you told me that you wanted to see me off because you had an urgent meeting with your delegate. I went home. The following day I learnt that you were at the dance, with a white girl. That's the man who swore on the dancing floor that he will love me till death.

"I don't think you had actually known exactly what kind of girl I am when you went about telling your drinking friends that I was an over ripe mango because I fell at the very first shake. You threw away a pearl, Fred, I tell you. Look at me Fred, I do not deceive myself, but I am beautiful, and I challenge you to enquire about me. I am single but I live a very decent life. Or you do not think I am beautiful enough for you to be proud of walking with me, sitting down with me and attending dances with me?"

He raised his eyes and met a baleful stare in hers.

"Of course you are beautiful," he said. "Otherwise why am I here now? As for finding out, I form my opinion of people, for better or for worse. I do not go around nosing and investigating. That is sending out the wrong signal."

"Op cush," she mimicked derisively through her nose. When I met you first I told myself, thank God, here comes a guy to be taken seriously. And when you invited me for the dance I came out of my shell, all to impress you. I threw myself at you. That's my way of loving, I do not do it haphazardly. I am either there or not. When you proposed friendship I asked you to give me time to think it over just as I am begging you now. You refused and so I yielded. I misjudged you and took you for a serious man because I thought there was something in you which I like to see in anybody I love or want to love. I can't tell you exactly what that is. The following day I was at your place to see you in the evening. They said you were out, but you were in and did not want to see me. You did not want to see me because I am too cheap."

Frederick sat up and told her:

"Although I have been silent all this while, it doesn't imply that I am guilty, that you are right in your allegations. All I will tell you is that when people fall in love, life does not come to a standstill. That happens only in films. Life moves on. You do not wear love like a shirt, you place on

38

the shelf and proceed with other activities. If I refuse to go to a dance with you but later attend the dance, you ought to understand what caused that change of mind. As in this case, it was my friend's girlfriend who was keen on attending the dance and we couldn't let her go alone. I obliged them and so went. We had a lot of important things to discuss and we did that even while the dance was going on. I don't see what else I could have done. Or it would have been better to take you to a dance and abandon you to carry out our discussions?"

"I have said more than that, Fred," she said with unreserved bitterness.

Her voice was calm but the professional side of Frederick sensed reserves of indignation building up inside her as she spoke, anxious to empty itself. Many years' experience in observing people in situations involving grief and grievances had taught him a valued lesson. If he were to convince her, he must remain silent, or at least not contradict her. He must let her give voice to her discontented feelings, however unjustified. In all fairness to him, the comment about shaking mangoes did not come from Frederick himself. It came from one of the gentlemen who had been trying very unsuccessfully to fall in love with Beatrice. Out of frustration he is said to have asked her:

"So you turned your back on us to follow a man who regards you as over-ripe mangoes that fall to the ground at the slightest shake." It sounded like the kind of comment Frederick could have made, but it was definitely taken out of context and could never have been referring specifically to Beatrice. At this moment it did not matter to her in what context the comment must have been made. It was sufficiently insulting.

"You make me feel ashamed, Beatrice," Frederick told her decisively. "It beats my imagination to hear you give such an answer – to me! One day you will discover, since you are so good at investigating, that despite my long association with women, my proposal to you was the very first in my life. I don't know whether that means anything to you."

She was not even listening anymore. She had gone to stand by the door as if to suggest that he should leave because his presence was making her more and more angry.

Disgust and disappointment were now blended on his countenance. His mind was even threatened with such an odd thing as laughter. But it settled down. No laughing matter, he thought. If he had come to tease her, knowing he did not care what her answer would be, he would have found the stomach to laugh it out. And he would have told her that her words could not wound him. He had not come to tease, he had come in deadly earnest to obtain only a "yes." She had given him a "No," the only "No" he ever received in his life. And at the moment when only a "Yes" mattered. Her refusal had come like a prickly pin to pierce and puncture the bubble of Frederick's hopes.

"It is not a sudden decision, Beatrice," he pointed out. "I have been thinking of it all along."

"But you should at least have made some sign. We are all adults. There is a way things can be communicated even without using words…"

"We needed to know each other well first, and that takes time."

"So according to you we have known each other well now. Is that what you want me to believe?"

"Of course."

She shook her head and as though she were the adult and Frederick the infant, she told him firmly: "We haven't at all. You have not known me. I have not known you…"

"I have known you," Frederick cut in."

"You haven't," she insisted. "If you really knew me you would have known that I cannot say 'yes' and you wouldn't even have asked me, especially when you are in a mad haste like this."

40

As though a stunning blow had been struck on the back of his head, he sat up, silently comprehending her answer. He could feel his feet freeze under him. This was unreal, untrue. False in all senses of the word. Could she possibly be refusing his offer? Could she possibly be telling him off? Not at this moment. He sighed deeply, repeatedly rearranged his position, and tried to relax as best he could while he pondered her answer over in his tortured mind.

"Whatever had happened in the past, Beatrice, let bygones be bygones. I am deadly serious now." His habitual pleasant voice was now thickened by the stress of his emotions and for the first time in his life he saw himself pleading.

"If you are deadly serious, Fred, I do not understand why you should be so anxious to get a reply now." And this was precisely the problem. Granted that Beatrice's memory for injury was phenomenal, granted that she had considered herself terribly scorned by Frederick, Beatrice was not incapable of letting bygones be bygones. In spite of all these grievances, she was beginning to come under Frederick's spell-binding personality. With only a little more time Beatrice would have fallen.

The situation in which Frederick found himself was not an easy one. At the tail end of the interview the Chairman had given him a warning:

"Dr. Ngenito, the members of this Commission who have been pleased to talk to you this morning are men of confidence, chosen by the state to do this all-important job. We do not find it necessary to tell you twice that whatever is transpiring between you and us has got to remain a closely guarded secret. No use creating unnecessary tension in the minds of the public."

And Frederick had given them his word, which they had no reason to doubt. Now he needed to reconsider that promise. Getting the job depended on getting married. And the way things were now, getting married depended on disclosing the secret. A kind of Catch 22.

"I need an answer urgently," he resumed. "It is a secret but you need to know it because it affects us both. I am just from an interview for the post of Director of Medical Services for the South West Province. There were several candidates but I was the most likely person except for the fact that I needed to be married. The Commission made me believe that the job is mine if I show up for the second and final phase of the interview with a marriage certificate."

That revelation shut the tiny door leading into her heart which she had already tried to open to permit Frederick a place. The revelation seemed to touch off a slow burning anger that immediately charged her thinking. What had lingered in the backwaters of her mind as a suspicion settled instantly into a conviction, an almost psychopathic fear of being used, a repulsion.

It is true that they had not actually known each other well enough to get married. Frederick seemed to hang on the fact that he was handsome, had a very respectable and enviable future. This was the bait that could attract most girls, but Beatrice was a very different type of person. She had an austere upbringing. Her father, a simple Catechist, had inculcated in her from infancy a peculiarly simple way of life: that the greatest wealth is content with little: a little house, a little family, a little food, a little ambition, a little everything. "It is not miserable to be in want of anything. It is miserable not to be able to bear the lack of it," she learnt that from her childhood. And she learned her lesson well – accepted that way of life as naturally as she accepted the seasons.

A strong believer in herself, she was never ashamed of going to school barefooted or wearing the same dress week in and week out, while others changed dresses like the chameleon changes its colours. If others laughed at her for what she looked like, she saw what they mocked and grinned too. And so she had grown up not really knowing or caring much about wealth, position, rank or pedigree. At a certain moment she considered entering the sisterhood but her mother begged her not to do so but to get married and have children to propagate the family blood. She had waited for ten years to decide to get married. When she met Frederick she felt the urge to get married. Something in her told her that a man like him could only marry a girl like her if his sense of judgement is right. But it was not a resolute resolve, however. She was twenty-five, but she could pass for a twenty year old, and her mirror had begun to warn her.

"So you want to marry me in order to become the Director of Medical Services, not so, Dr. Frederick Ngenito?"

Perspiration beaded his forehead and neck so that he undid the first button and pulled open his tie and left it hanging loosely on his chest.

"Fred, let me tell you from my little experience that I cannot get married for this kind of reason. I know I am old enough to get married. I know I will get married. But it cannot be for this reason. What will you do with me if tomorrow you are no longer the Director?"

"You will marry me for what reason?'

"I didn't say that I will marry you... I know myself."

Dazed, dry-mouthed, sick to his stomach, Frederick pulled himself to his feet and wobbled out into the street.

Chapter Six

The road was just about ten metres from Beatrice's little house. A few metres from the house Frederick could have signalled to one of the numerous taxis that passed. But he chose to walk a good distance, cocking his ears and, against his better judgement, hoping to hear Beatrice recant and call for him back. Instead, as soon as he stepped down the roadside she banged the door behind. He kept walking until the road turned the corner such that he could no longer see the house, then he took a taxi away.

Frederick was a man with a very analytical mind and usually when confronted with a problem he took his time to weigh its full implications. He did not regard his loss of Beatrice as a calamity or even a misfortune, painful as it was. Like the fox in the legendary tale of the sour grapes, he tried to look at it differently, he tried to rationalise the situation. He told himself that the office of Director was not his in the first place. He now began to wonder why they would use such an unscientific and unprofessional clause as marriage to decide his fate as Director of Medical Services. It was possible that the Commission had somebody else in mind and were just looking for a pretext. If Beatrice accepted him and he showed up at the second interview with a marriage certificate, they would find some other excuse to reject him. Perhaps that was why providence had stepped in to save him the embarrassment right from the start by making Beatrice refuse his offer. Otherwise he could not understand what he had done so wrong that she would reject him so vociferously.

He would get even with them. He would make them see that he was not even interested in the office. The office of Director, he reasoned, was a political appointment which could be taken away at any time. He had not trained as a medical doctor and specialised in Topical Medicine and surgery to return and sign meaningless documents. He had been trained to come back and cure people, to carry out research and perform experiments that would help improve the lot of mankind. From that perspective, he saw Beatrice's refusal as a blessing in disguise although she had not done so wittingly.

There were two other passengers inside the taxi he had taken.

"Where is oga going?" the baffled driver asked.

"Take me to Raymond," he said.

"Raymond, sa?"

"To Barombi Kang," Fred corrected himself, "Agric Post."

"Am not going out of town, sa, unless on hire," the driver told him politely.

"Hire is how much?"

"Two thousand francs, sa."

"O.K, go, I will pay you that."

They travelled a hundred yards and then the driver asked the irate passengers to drop and look for another taxi. They did so, cursing and complaining, although they were near their destination and would easily walk there and save the money.

It was lunch time when he arrived Raymond's place, but he did not join the family at table. As soon as he knocked and entered, Raymond rose and, shaking his hand vigorously announced:

"Mr. Provincial Director! When is your installation and how did it go?"

Fred smiled, shook his head and said: "a very interesting day. Nothing to write home about."

Raymond was no relative of Fred, just a friend, but they had lived like brothers for over thirty years. He came from an entirely different tribe, the Ibulongs. The two of them first met in the house of a certain Cosmas Weeleng, an uncle to Fred and a friend to Raymond's own father. Fred was older than him by a year, and also more brilliant. Educators were very rare in those days, and Weelang was not an ordinary teacher, he was a headmaster. And not only that, he was known to be a very stern disciplinarian, by which they meant that he could inflict merciless physical punishment on any child who committed an offence. In the spirit of the age, parents tended to equate sternness with sound education. Cosmas Weeleng was reputed for being a disciplinarian and the only intellectual who could "drill book into a child's head." Until the end of his life Fred was never to learn convincingly about what actually prompted his father to send him to live with such a man. Whenever he asked his father the old man would simply say:

"Your mother would have spoilt you completely, and she did not like to see me punish you."

He said Fred's mother petted him far too much. But although Weelang did help in moulding him, his sternness went dangerously close to making him and Raymond develop criminal tendencies. Because they were usually given very little to eat, they developed the habit of stealing food and even money in order to feed themselves. Woe betide a visitor who came to the house and hung his coat carelessly, they would empty it of the pennies and even shillings. This was no way to bring up children. Weelang did worse than that: Fred and Raymond were excellent footballers, young as they were. Weelang hated children who played football and did everything to discourage the idea in them. On the day that they were to play a match with another school, Weelang would mix six cups of rice in six cups of garri and ask the boys to sort them, making sure that the quantities remained the same at the end. The boys would miss the game. When this information got to the sports master, the man decided to send other pupils to help them separate the rice from the garri so that they would participate in the game. But when this proved unsuccessful and the boys often finished too late to be useful, the man came up with a brighter idea: he bought six cups of rice and six cups of garri and gave to the boys. They put the rice and garri in their separate containers and went off to play, having dumped what Weelang gave them into a pit latrine. On their return they were given a snake beating. Although Weelang always gave six cups each, on that fateful day, he ran short of rice and so measured only four cups. How was it that he now had six cups? Another snake beating resulted

Fred believed that Weelang's contribution was slight and that he could still have made it in life had he never gone to live with the man. In the High School and the University he was a key striker in the football team, an activity which brought him much honour, money and many girls. And that was the talent Weelang was bent on destroying! As a result of the inhuman treatment they received, he vowed that when he grew up and had children, none of them would ever be sent to live with anybody else outside his home. Thus he made it in spite of Weelang. Because of the pleasure he took in beating up the boys, they called him "Casingo" behind his back. "Casingo" was another word for the cane.

Fred and Raymond left Weelang's house immediately they wrote their Standard Six Examination. They then found themselves together in Sasse College where they lived together for five years. They went to the High School from Sasse and there they began to separate. Raymond, more interested in making quick money entered the Agricultural Training sector of the High School where they were considered as civil servants on training and earned a substantial stipend. He later did a degree after so many years in the field, in Agricultural Science in the National Polytechnic.

But the richest and most eventful period of their lives in terms of excitement and adventure shared together, seemed to be their days in the "Casingo" household. Even as adults, the two of them were never tired of telling stories about their days in "Casingo's" house. When "Casingo" married, his wife was joined soon afterwards by a cousin, Ferdinand. He was the third boy with whom they served "Casingo." Ferdinand was a virtual moron who soon became the butt of all their pranks. "Casingo" could be said to have drilled book into the heads of Raymond and Fred. He had a library of forty-seven books which he compelled the boys to read and make summaries. This was not a hard-and-fast rule, but only a way of keeping the boys at home. The boys first came into contact with some of the world's classics in "Casingo,s" library: these included *Robinson Cruse, Treasure Island, Kidnapped, John Plough Man, Macbeth* (the boys nicknamed his wife Lady Macbeth!), *She stoops to conquer, Mutiny on the bounty*, amongst others. When the boys discovered that "Casingo" himself had not read up to ten of the books they began to forge stories as contents of books they read from the library.

This exercise became very useful to them when they entered Sasse College. There, Father Cunningham, the famous principal and renowned educationist, instituted the rule of reading and making summaries. Students in the lower forms were required to read a book a week and submit the title, the author, the publisher, date and place of publication along with a one-page summary every Saturday evening, to their Literature teacher who read and graded the submissions and returned the books by the following Tuesday. Fred and Raymond scarcely ever read any books. They simply recalled tales from "Casingo's" library and submitted, always scoring very good marks.

With Ferdinand "Casingo" met with complete failure when he discovered for the first time and in his own house, that certain children are born dull, are unteachable and should be best left alone or a different career chosen for them that had nothing to do with academics. Raymond and Fred usually recalled with a lot of amusement an attempt on the part of Weelang to teach Ferdinand Arithmetic. Weelang would begin by telling him the answers:

"Ferdinand, two plus two equals four."

"Two plus two equals four," Ferdinand would repeat. After rehearsing for about five minutes, Weelang would then put him to the test:

"Ferdinand, what is two plus two?"

Ferdinand would reflect for a while, having already forgotten the answer, and then would say:

"Equals."

"Equals what?" Weelang would scream at him.

"Equals two," he would say trembling and in response to which Weelang would immediately pull out his "casingo" and lash him six strokes. That usually changed nothing because Ferdinand still gave the same ridiculous answer.

Then there was the idea of story-telling which Weelang thought he should inculcate in the boys. Every Saturday evening at about eight o'clock, Radio Nigeria Enugu broadcast a short story. Weelang loved the programme and decided that the children must also love it. He would compel them to listen to the story. At the end of the radio broadcast he would ask each of them to retell the story as read over the radio, and then he would ask each of them to tell his own story, any story at all. The first part of the exercise was generally manageable for Ferdinand who only needed to recall a few names and places and a particular episode. It was in the second part involving the fabrication of a story that Ferdinand usually got stuck. When it came to Ferdinand's turn he would say something like:

"One time there was a man and three children. One day the man asked them to tell a story each. The first child said…." At this point he would retell to Weelang's chagrin, the story which either Fred or Raymond had just told, or what he could recall from the story. He never succeeded in telling a story of his own. By far, his most dramatic coup remained the incident when he topped his class for a few hours. It was the last day of the third term and, knowing that the boys were anxious to go to their parents, he announced that morning: "Anybody who comes first in his class will be free to go to his parents on holidays."

When they returned that afternoon Ferdinand caused a great stir when he announced very confidently that he had come first in his class. When Weelang asked to see his progress report, he saw one quite all right, but there had been some scratching and the position was not *1st* but *1 th*, with a gap between the *1* and the *th.* .

"How many of you were in your class?" Weelang asked Ferdinand.

"Nineteen," he answered.

Ferdinand had come last, but, anxious to return to his parents, he had simply erased the figure 9. He had thus frauded. Casingo!

When Weelang married Madam Angellina, the boys rejoiced because they thought her presence would make life more comfortable as she would do the cooking while they would only eat. But she turned out to be a very mean and vicious woman who made life virtually unbearable especially for Raymond and Frederick. She served Ferdinand's food separately from the other boys whose food was served in one plate. Thus she was able to feed her cousin satisfactorily while the two other boys were given just enough to prevent them from dying of starvation. On her part, she had a glutton's appetite and would empty a basket of bread meant for ten persons or more. Whenever they had visitors, which was the moment when house boys generally had a field day, Madam Angel would leave the guests at table and follow a boy who had just carried the remains from a visitor's plate

51

into the kitchen where she would warn him to put the plates in the cupboard until she had examined them, examining them meant licking them and chewing the bones.

She seemed to take much pleasure in seeing Fred and Raymond beaten by her husband. She would trump up a charge against the boys – they insulted the mother of a passer-by or answered her rudely – and immediately suggest how many strokes of the cane the culprit should be given. One sad fact was that Weelang never doubted her evidence, he never tried to verify the truth about anything she accused them of. Initially, the two boys had discovered a way of saving their skin: they would stuff their buttocks with pieces of cloth when they anticipated punishment. That way, the strokes never actually touched their bodies even though they would scream as if the cane had wounded them. One day Madam Angel discovered the trick and immediately reported to Weelang that the boys had become more stubborn because they knew that they would stuff their buttocks with sheets which would make it impossible for them to feel the pain.

Thereafter Weelang stripped the boys naked before beating them. An embarrassing fact about Raymond was that, being from a family that was naturally very hairy, he developed pubic hair very early, much earlier than his friend. Whenever they were stripped naked for beating, she would crawl up and sit down staring at the area between the boy's legs and say:

"Look at that Raymond, he is already looking like an adult, but still doing things like a child."

Even in school, Weelang practised his fiendish cruelty without restraint. He would be teaching such an easy subject as Writing when he would suddenly hear a teacher next door beating up pupils for some offence committed. Not to be outdone, Weelang would suddenly switch from Writing to Weather Observation or Arithmetic where he was bound to come up with a culprit.

"Show me your Weather Observation books," he would order, brandishing his "casingo," his eyes flaming with instant anger. He would then fall on pupils who were still planning to go home during long break and fetch their books, just for the joy of it.

He had some redeeming features, however, although they could never outweigh or even remotely justify his cruelty. For instance, he hated lies and would punish anyone severely if he was discovered to have told a lie. This insistence on the truth helped mould the boys into very honest beings. They started off by fearing to tell lies because of the punishment that awaited them upon discovery. Then it became a way of life as they grew up. But sometimes the boys were forced to tell lies just because of the man's severe nature. One such occasion took place one day when Raymond decided that their flask was dirty enough to deserve washing. When Weelang returned from school and noticed the flask standing on its mouth he nodded and called for the boys.

"Who washed this flask and put it upside down like this?" he queried. Actually he wanted to congratulate whoever did it and to encourage them to use their initiative a lot more often. But the tone of his voice made the boys think that there was something wrong. Not wanting to be punished alone, Raymond said:

"I washed the flask, sir, but it was Fred who wiped it and put it upside down."

"Don't call my name," Fred said, not anxious to share in his friend's crime. "I did not even see the flask, sir," he continued. When it was finally established that Raymond washed the flask alone, "casingo," for daring to tell lies against his friend.

Another thing which infuriated Weelang very much was unnecessary noise making or shouting. Raymond and Fred always teamed up to cause Ferdinand to fall foul of this law. They recalled an occasion on which Madam Angellina gave Ferdinand a sweet. As soon as he peeled the sweet from the paper covering and put in his mouth, Fred and his friend fell on him and tickled him so violently that in an attempt to shout he swallowed the sweet. Because he had meant to enjoy its sweetness by sucking it for a longer time, Ferdinand then started crying, inviting the angry attention of Weelang who immediately asked him what had happened.

"He swallowed his sweet, sir, and then began to cry," Raymond said.

"You took his sweet or he swallowed it?"

"He swallowed it," Fred insisted.

'Ferdinand, did anybody take your sweet?"

"No, sir."

"You swallowed it, not so?"

"Yes, sir," the poor boy admitted.

Casingo!

Sometimes, Fred and his friend deliberately misled Ferdinand just to ensure that he remained permanently stupid. On days that Weelang announced that they would be tested on World Affairs or Civics in the evening, Fred and Raymond would invite Ferdinand to join them in revision. Weelang was generally interested in Heads of State and Capital cities, so Raymond would do the interrogation.

"What is the Capital City of Ghana?"

"Kwame Nkrumah," Fred would say.

"Correct," Raymond would say.

"What is the Capital City of Nigeria?"

"Abubakar Tafawa Belewa."

"Correct."

"Who is the Prime Minister of England?"

"Australia."

"Correct. Clap for yourself."

Raymond would then turn to Ferdinand with the same questions. He would answer just the way Fred had answered.

"Correct," Raymond would say. "Clap for yourself."

Later that evening they would sit back to listen to Ferdinand invite several "casingos" with his ridiculous answers, while they themselves gave the right answers to any questions asked.

Fred refused a beer, preferring ordinary water. The fact that he refused to eat or drink and sat speechlessly, and without his usually gaiety forced Raymond to rush over his meal and come to join him.

"Tell me, doc, exactly what happened."

The dining table was to the right of where he was sitting, slightly behind him. He leaned back slightly and glanced at Mariana, Raymond's wife still eating, indicating that he did not want her to follow what he had to say. Raymond understood, lighted a cigarette, his curse, and they went to sit on cane chairs at the far corner of his long veranda.

"Ray, the interview itself was nothing," Fred began gravely.

"How do you mean?"

"It was all child's play. Nothing that I expected..."

"I told you it would be just conversation. And then?"

"And then they asked me to get married and possess a legal document to that effect before the second and last interview which comes up in a fortnight."

Raymond nodded, took in a long breath and lay back, pulling at his cigarette. After a while he rose again and said:

"That sounds like a hard one, doc. But we will see how it goes. If all else fails, we get somebody to fake a marriage certificate for us and you carry there. After all, they do not need to see your wife physically."

Fred smiled at the ingenuity and said: "I hope it never comes to that. But, Ray, I was wondering as I came, why they needed two interviews."

"To claim the sitting fees. Do you know how much each of those blokes will be paid just for today?"

Fred shook his head in the negative.

"At least fifty thousand francs," Raymond said. "There used to be four or five interviews for the same candidates, for the same reason. But the Government felt ashamed and cut it down to two. It might one day boil down to one interview for whatever job."

"From the interview I went straight to that our lady's place."

"Beatrice?"

"Yaa."

"What for?" Raymond asked. "You should have waited until you had been appointed before taking the news to her. Anyway, what happened?"

"I proposed to her and she refused."

"You did what and she did what?"

"You heard me well," Fred said.

"Did she know why you were proposing?"

Fred nodded. "I told her," he said.

"And she still refused?"

Fred nodded and smiled, it was full of embarrassment, not from the heart.

Raymond too smiled. He wanted to blame Fred for rushing the proposal but he decided not to rub it in. Instead, he laid the blame on Beatrice. He said: "I always knew she was a very very difficult girl, as I told you. But I didn't think that in addition to being complicated, she was also blind, blind to the prospects that such a marriage offered for her. That's interesting, that's really interesting."

"It really is," Fred said resignedly.

"She is just making life more and more difficult for herself and for everybody else," Raymond said and went on to remind Fred of the fairy tale they heard in the primary school about a head, which Fred had long forgotten. In that tale, there was a woman who thought she was so beautiful that she turned away all her suitors. One day a handsome man appeared and won her admiration and her hand and took her away. As they went along people jumped from various corners to reclaim his body parts: the man who had lent him a shoulder came for it, so did the man who had lent him the belly, the back, the legs, and so on, until in the end he was left only with what he owned from the start, a head.

"Looks like that's what she is waiting for quite all right," Fred said. "But I cannot believe, I do not see myself being rebuffed by a woman."

"But she has done so, following what you have said."

"But that is not the end of the story," Fred said. "Never say never."

"I am with you, doc," Raymond said. "We just have to fish around for someone else."

"I don't see her getting away with it," Fred said with great resolve and determination.

Chapter Seven

Frederick was the first son of Chief Mutare, a man of many parts, a man who could only be described as an embodiment of oddities. But Frederick was never to be called Prince because of the dubious circumstances under which his father had seized on the title of Chief. He was not of the royal line. The title came about when their tribesmen were few in Kumba and held their family meetings every Sunday in his house. He was the President of the group and represented them at the Kumba Municipal Council meetings. The title actually came from the Council which soon began to call him the chief of the Lemoh-Begoas. The man loved the title to the extent that he soon began to take offence at anybody who called him by any other title. He ordered a traditional gown and headgear, or rather, traditional gowns and head-gears with a red feather and two porcupine spikes stuck together on the right side. He also ordered a special walking stick made. He bought a beautiful velvet mat which Moslems squatted on during prayers. This he would spread or cause to be spread in kingly fashion over the chair in which he was going to sit, just as the traditional rulers usually did. In the beginning he carried the cloth himself, but as his title took root he had a small boy or a tribesman carry it for him whenever he was invited to an occasion. He was very glad when one of his sons, Fred's kid brother, offered to carry it about with him. His people were not terribly disturbed because it was a harmless title, he was not rivalling with anybody, did not constitute a threat, although he had been warned by the Paramount Chief of their clan at home not to wear his kingly paraphernalia in his presence.

Down in the Coast which meant Muyuka, Mutengene and Victoria, he could call himself anything and get away with it. And he did. As chiefs usually did, he refused to shake hands, an act which got on people's nerves. But he was a very generous old man, especially when it came to defending his title. He was never tired of giving drinks to his cronies. He so cherished the title that unknown to his people, he applied to the Ministry of Territorial Administration to be named a third class chief. He had a strong case and a heavy purse to do the fighting and one day the radio authenticated what began like a big joke. The traditional rulers from his area protested and once when a Paramount Chief died whom he knew personally and was friendly to, and he appeared with his entourage to mourn for the man, the other chiefs rebelled and left the canopy that had been set aside for the chiefs. It took several hours for the District Officer to explain and convince the chiefs that it was the man's right to sit amongst the chiefs. In the end they were forced to admit him or, at best, simply ignored him, thus strengthening his claims to the title.

Once people were getting used to addressing him Chief, Mutare did everything to live like the conventional Chiefs. He even surrounded himself with more pomp than many Paramount Chiefs who used to poke fun at him back home. In every palace back home, there were festivities in the palace at the end of every market day. There, the market days were not fixed, but rotated every week, Monday this week, Tuesday next week, Wednesday the third week, and so on. In K-Town, the market day was Saturday. Chief Mutare soon instituted traditional dances every Saturday evening. Although the initial intention was to impress on his people the idea of Chieftaincy, those Saturday night shows served a very important cultural purpose in that they exposed children and young men born and bred in K-Town to aspects of their culture which they would have witnessed only in the village. The most important dance on such occasions was the "brumbrum," a very energetic and strenuous dance. The dancers were generally healthy and agile young men in their twenties or early thirties, who usually had the muscles of body builders. Their upper bodies and their feet were bare, but they covered their buttocks and the entire waist area with loincloths tied tightly round the waists and reaching down to the knees. Usually, eight persons danced at a time in two lines of four, one behind the other. Responding to the vigorous thumping of the drums and xylophones, they would march with quick steps, sword in hand or sometimes with pieces of wood carved and painted to look like swords, halt abruptly and jump high up into the air until you saw their underpants, land simultaneously with a squat, spin round in that squatting position as they flexed and unflexed their muscles, before jumping back to their feet to continue the gruelling exercise.

On such occasions Chief Mutare dressed formally, like a real Chief anywhere: on his head he wore a cotton cap made of natural-coloured and indigo blue cotton yarn in looping technique. Decorated with cowries and blue cylindrical beads on the front, the cap was lined with yellow felt-like fabric on the front and back. Round his neck were two rows of jewellery made from the inner part of raffia bast and embroidered with black, white, light and dark blue, and yellow beads. These were allowed to fall over his padded jacket made of red and white gauze-like light fabric padded with cotton, with an inner lining of checkered European cloth. Under this he wore a loose pair of trousers made from black linen with double gongs, hearts and lizards embroidered primarily in the colours red, white and yellow. On his feet were slippers of dyed hide decorated with red, yellow and white patches. He would sit on a high throne-like stool with each of his two wives standing on either side, carrying fly whisks, one white and the other black. In front of him usually stood a low stool covered with bead-embroidered cloth carrying the image of a leopard intertwined with a double-headed snake in dark, medium and light blue colours and reaching right down to the base of the stool. On the stool usually stood a calabash covered with cane plaiting up to the onset of the neck which was decorated with little rectangular metal pieces that were pounded into the neck in checkered pattern. It had a fibre stopper with cotton cloth sewn around it and from it his "nchinda" who always stood at the ready, poured palm wine into his buffalo horn.

As the dancers danced and the drummers drummed, Chief Mutare nodded to the rhythm of the music, swayed from side to side in kingly fashion. At the climax of the display, Chief Mutare would thrust his hand into his handbag and pull out a handful of coins which he would give to his servant, his "nchinda," who would go and distribute to the dancers amidst great rejoicing. Young men and even neighbours, craving for more, always enjoyed the spectacle and looked forward to another Saturday night. And the women would retire to their homes singing praises to Chief Mutare.

Chief Mutare, now in his late seventies, had fought in Burma during the Second World War where he served as an ambulance driver and later as a nursing aid to take care only of the blacks for it was inconceivable that a black man would give medicine to a sick or wounded or dying white man. That was tantamount to poisoning him. He told stories of how cruelly they were treated. He said they were returning from a family meeting one day when a police vehicle stopped them and seized the able-bodied men amongst them. They were trained for a week and then given guns. They were to carry the guns and observe the white man use it for one month before attempting to use it. He said in just one day they had all acquired the skill of manipulating the guns and fired with greater accuracy than most of the so-called white masters. He said that because the white masters had no faith in their competence they were not given challenging tasks and as a result they spent much time loafing around in the camps, doing the dirty jobs – cleaning the latrines, emptying buckets of excrement and washing dishes and clothing. They were forbidden to cook. This he said, was how he came to know so much about diagnosing patients and administering drugs. Mutare was barely literate. He had gone to school already an adult, mainly to be able to record the names of people owing him and the amounts. So he could barely read and write, skills he sharpened on the warfront. Because they were generally neglected he spent time reading up medical magazines and other health and Do-It-Yourself books.

He told the story of how they managed to abandon camp. He said that the war in Burma required more tact than force and so, in the opinion of the white masters, the black man was not very much needed. He usually came in as cannon fodder on whom the enemy was encouraged to waste its bullets. Without too much to do many of them were bored with camp life. One day a friend hatched a trick: he pretended he was suddenly blind. The head of their unit was accordingly informed and he took a quick decision: the blind man was to be sent back to his country for visual incapacity. Five others followed suit with the same complaint and were also discharged from the army and sent back home.

Mutare and three others who showed up for an eye test were not that lucky. The growing number of blind people, especially amongst the blacks alarmed the unit leaders who informed the hierarchy. A female ophthalmologist-cum-psychiatrist arrived to take care of the problem. She quickly established that most if not all those who had been discharged were not sick at all but were just pretending. On the day Mutare and his fellow *blind* men showed up, the woman sat on the stage in a large hall where she decided to do her consultation. She was stark naked, facing the blind men who had been stripped to their underpants in readiness for the medical examinations. She knew that any truly blind man would not be disturbed by her nakedness, since he would not be able to see. The ploy worked: as soon as they were led into the hall and they looked across at the spectacle on the stage, all the blind men including Mutare escaped and returned to their posts, declaring that they had miraculously regained their sight. Nobody ever tried again to pretend to be blind. Those who had attempted to trick the unit leadership were severely punished. That was why Mutare was one of the very last persons to return home. But his long stay, even though it worried members of his family, paid off because he continued to deepen his knowledge of medicine in the medical dispensary with the badly wounded, the slightly wounded and the mortally wounded.

When he returned to a hero's welcome, his language larded with fragments of German, French and English words (mostly insults), it was quickly noticed that there were several vital screws missing from his head. Having spent three or four years receiving orders blindly and dishing out some blindly, keeping company only with men in the last stages of agony, where he could only keep people quiet by shouting, he became a social problem. He behaved with the rashness of somebody on the warfront, always acting before reflecting, unyielding, a strong believer in his own judgement, and unwilling to be talked out of his decision, hated being contradicted, however nonsensical his view of a situation. He used his fist more often than was necessary in solving domestic problems and his wives lived in absolute terror of him. He drank a lot but drink had nothing to do with his uncouth behaviour since he was just as wild without drink.

Chief Mutare was the very incarnation of brute force, raw, untouched either by surface culture or inner human feelings. His was primitive force arrogantly striking the eye like a huge boulder in the middle of a field. And, like a boulder, it was in its own way expressive. He ruled his house by decrees. He would declare: "No meat for seven days," and for seven days nobody would taste meat. If it was suspected that anybody ate meat during that period, such a person received a thorough beating. Some months he would declare a month of family mourning for all the family members that had died. He would shave his hair and wear black clothes for one month, compelling others to do the same. It was a security risk to disagree with him on any issue, including even the weather. He was physically very strong, a fact that was reinforced by his training and exercises in the army. And in the hospital where he served until he retired he was feared by everybody, including the doctors.

His face was coarse, with high cheekbones and a low forehead, very prominent, arched eyebrows and narrow eyes that looked out wickedly. His hands were unusually long and powerful like a gorilla's. Whenever he was angry, and that was very often, he could be seen clenching his fingers with their work-knotted knuckles, into a fist. He would hold them that way for a while as if he were clutching someone by the throat, then unclench them quickly to clench them again slowly.

He was just around 1.75 metres tall, the same height with Frederick, but enormously muscular even in his seventies. He was light in complexion and had two large, conspicuous tattoos of a dragon and a scorpion, one on each arm. He always kept the tattoos hidden. To see them you had to provoke him severely because they were hidden on his upper arm. To make them visible he would have to roll up his sleeves. But sometimes he wore sleeveless *jumpas* which exposed his upper arm.

Notwithstanding, on the credit side his knowledge of the human anatomy was so thorough that doctors were not ashamed to consult him on certain thorny issues before, during or after an operation. They in the medical sector in the warfront had worked with corpses which were cut up and examined in every detail to understand the functioning of the human body and because he found this better than firing guns in the frontlines, he achieved very great competence in the exercise. For any kind of surgical operation, he knew how to select the necessary instruments and line them up in the order in which they would be required for use in the course of the operation. On that score, for once, his actions were predictable and impressive. Few doctors carried out an operation without him and there were some who postponed an operation just because the old man was not in town. In spite of his age his hands were unusually steady, something very rare for a system which imbibed so much alcohol.

He was just a simple staff nurse, but his knowledge of medicine was phenomenal and many people thought his life was fulfilled when they heard that his very brilliant son, Frederick had developed an interest in medicine where he was doing very well. He never took "no" for an answer. In fact, in many quarters he was called "Doctor Chief," or "Pa Doctor." The reason being that whenever he was on duty he never allowed a doctor to give up on a patient. He committed abortions and performed D & Cs with a hundred percent success even in his house where he ran a small dispensary. Frederick took an interest in medicine from helping him in his small lab at home. He was not scared by the sight of blood and quite often in the dead of night patients could be heard screaming their lungs out in pain from his little dispensary.

He had an old motor cycle, a Royal Enfield with the familiar roaring sound of a rocket about to blast off. He called it his "iron horse" with which he performed great feats: he could ride it for a fifty metres with his hands held high above his head; he could ride it for a hundred metres on its back wheel, the front wheel raised into the air. It was a single-cylinder engine. He used it to ferry his clients to their destinations after attending to them late at night. Once after an accident he amputated a leg at the knee without using any anaesthetic. It permitted him to bind the wound and stop the bleeding which seemed unstoppable. As the victim continued to scream Pa picked up the leg and slammed on the stretcher next to him and shouted: "I hear one more cough from you I will stitch this leg back and cut it again, several times."

The man calmed down. He could not face the possibility of having his leg cut twice. Once was painful enough.

Chief Mutare was a polygamist with three wives. Fred's mother was his first wife. When she died he exclaimed at the height of his grief, to the hearing of the women, friends and relatives:

"Papa God, how can you do this to me? You leave all these toads to snore round me in the night and only choose this my golden egg?"

His opinions were as changeable as the Buea weather. Sunshine this minute and rain the next. If he was angry with you he would tell you every bad thing he had ever heard about you. And if you happened to do something that pleased him, he would swear you were the only good person on earth. He would place you alongside the great saints. He would just as easily forget all your goodness if you hurt him. Among his oddities was a dagger he always carried with him. He said he carried it for self defence but he could very easily use it for offence. When he assumed the title of Chief he ordered a baton which was actually a concealed dagger which he carried about as the staff of office.

His endlessly unpredictable nature made it difficult for his daughters to get married. Suitors were scared of him, and with good reason. . If he found a boy hovering around his compound, he threatened him with death. If he found a boy or even a gentleman talking to any of his daughters he could draw his sword. Thus he was stuck with five grown up daughters. Once when a neighbour with whom he once had some land dispute visited him with his wife, bringing food and drinks to ask for one of his daughters' hands for their son who was also present, the old man listened to them and then rose and addressed the visitor:

"You steal my land and then you come with rotten food and drinks to deceive me into giving out my daughter for marriage into such a family? Have you replaced the *Nkeng* which you displaced from the boundary? Or you think I have forgotten? Get out of my house before I sharpen a cutlass on you."

The people left humiliated, the girl, Irene, whose hand they had come to ask for, was in tears for a week, at the end of which she asked the father:

"Papa, you want to marry me? You send away everybody who comes to see you concerning me. I hope you will take care of the children I will soon begin to deliver in this house." She did actually give him two bastard sons in three years. But the old man remained unrepentant.

"When the right man comes I shall give you out," he said. "For you to get married to thieves and vagabonds, you better remain in this house and deliver those children you are threatening to deliver."

He had long gone on retirement, but ever since he was in the service, whenever South Westerners complained of never having had one of their children as the Director of Medical Services, he used to tell them:

"I am preparing my son for that office."

And when the plane carrying Dr. Karin Karin, the former Director ran into bad weather on his way to attending a WHO meeting in Congo Kinshasa crashed in the forest of the Congo killing all on board, he said it was the will of God. He was never afraid of speaking the truth, or what to him was the truth. It was the very first time the office had been vacant and was likely to be filled by a South Westerner.

It did not matter to him that the appointment had to be made from above. He knew how much influence he wielded in the society and how easily he could rally people to come to his aid in defence of a worthy cause. He was not above storming into the ministry of health to make sure that his son was given his due. As a matter of fact, it was especially because of the fear of the unknown that the Commission was so anxious to make sure that Frederick got the job.

"We will all march to Yaounde and see the Prime Minister," he said, "if they do not give us that post."

He outlined what he knew to be the special advantages of being Director before Frederick left home in the morning: he is a key member of the Board that selects candidates for the Medical School, Nursing institutes; he runs a budget and can cause hospitals or health centres to be opened in every corner of their province; in only one year he can flood the hospitals with nurses and drugs. The reason the South West still lagged behind the other provinces so woefully was because they had never had their own child in a power position to cause things to happen. The time had finally come. He can open a hospital in the village and with the hospital development follows automatically. It was not an office to trifle with.

*****

This was the atmosphere into which Dr. Frederick Ngenito was bringing the news that the vital document would not be had before the deadline passed and that he might lose the job. This was the warped mind to which Frederick was bringing his *laissez-faire* philosophy towards the office of Director of Medical Services for the South West. He had better brace himself for a confrontation well nigh a third world war!

Chapter Eight

Chief Mutare was sitting in the veranda of his home with legs stretched out on the adjustable extension of the lounge chair, enjoying the warm weather. It was something to cherish because the rains had been heavy lately and, even though women and farmers who had just planted their seeds rejoiced, it made travelling difficult and life miserable. On a large cane side stool stood a bottle of Schnapps and a four-litre jug of fresh palm wine which he tapped himself. His horn was in his right hand. When he noticed Frederick coming from the distance (the man had formidable eyesight!) he poured himself a good quantity of palm wine, spiced it up with some Schnapps, drank it all in one gulp and replaced the horn on his leather bag on the stool. He moved his dagger closer to the foot of the lounge chair. Frederick had hardly stepped into the compound when he enquired:

"How did it go, son of man?" He was beaming with pride because he knew or believed that the mission could only succeed. Yet there was some trace of anxiety, of fear in the tone of his question. It was as if he also feared that things could go some other way that would not favour them.

"Pa, won't you let me come first into the house?" Fred spoke wearily, truly tired.

"It is to show you how I am thinking about it," the old man said. "You think if I met you up the road I would not ask you but wait until we got home? Is it theft? Did I send you to go and steal? I sent you to go and take what is yours by right. Tell me what I want to hear. My friends are waiting for me to bring them the news. You saw the people, son?"

"I did, father. I was there from nine o'clock to eleven. But I left them a very long time ago as you can see…"

"I have told you over and over that good news is like a treasure in your bag. You do not carry it about. You bring it home to your father to share it out. How did it go?"

"Fine, or what should I say?"

"I don't like the way you are looking. See how you are trembling like you are going to tell a lie. They said they will take you?"

There was silence before Frederick said:

"Yes and no."

"Why are you talking like a witch doctor who has encountered a disease he cannot cure but cannot give back people's money? They told you 'yes and no?' Tell me what I want to hear."

"They will take me. They gave me the assurance that they will take me. They told me how useful you have been to them and how they hope I would be the same."

"Of course you will surpass all I did. I achieved all that with bare hands. Now there is everything at your disposal. You did not tell them that You will do open heart surgery here? You did not tell them that…."

"Pa, let me finish. The only fly in the ointment is that I should be a married man. They have had to reschedule another interview just so that I can get married."

"Married?" Not that Chief Mutare was surprised that they should want his son to be married. He was exclaiming at the fact that an important position like that of Director should depend on such a slight condition as marriage.

"They say I should be married," he said again and shook his head when the thought of what had just transpired between him and Beatrice crossed his mind.

"Then the job is ours," his father said, "if marriage is the thing. How many wives do they want you to produce?"

"One," he replied from deep down his throat.

"My son, are you not grateful to God that the herbs they are asking for to cure the whole tribe are growing right at your own doorsteps?" He smiled and served himself a drink. He put the Schnapps first in the horn and then held the horn for Frederick to pour the palm wine into it. As he replaced the jug and sat back he said:

"I am thankful to God, father. But the point is that I don't think it will be as easy as that for me to get married. I think I have not found a girl I could get married to, yet."

Chief Mutare flung the horn at his son and some of the drink touched him before the horn fell to the ground, spilling the rest. He threw his right hand on the side stool and the jug of palm wine fell to the ground along with the bottle of Schnapps. Frederick, his faithful son who had never done anything to offend his father, rose and lifted the jug before it emptied itself on the cement floor. He also took the bottle of Schnapps and replaced on the table. Then he picked up the horn and wiped it before showing it to his father.

"Go fo before, fo back. Is that not how the record sings?"

He was definitely not enjoying himself. He was visibly angry. He seized the horn from Frederick and threw on the stool, munching his lower lip, his eyes turning red. Something in him told him that it was too early to get angry. The door, as his people would say, was still far off, so he could not afford to start bending from a distance else his back would ache before the real moment of bending came. He allowed his nerves to calm down for a while and then he enquired softly:

"What do you mean by finding a girl to get married to? Are you talking about a girl that would fall from the sky with a marriage certificate bearing your name as her husband? You marry one, if you are not satisfied you marry another and another. Is it the feeding that you lack? I had your mother, may she rest in peace, and after that I married two other women. If I had more room I would marry a fourth and why not a fifth? I do not understand you, sincerely, my son, I do not understand you. When people travel with wood ash in their bags like you, they leave a trail which only those like us who come later see it. You do not know how much people are discussing you and Afesseh's daughter. What's that her name now…?"

"Beatrice."

"Yes, Beatrice. A woman like that will be good enough for the Director," he laughed loudly and asked Frederick to serve him another drink. He held his horn and allowed him to put first the palm wine and then the Schnapps. Then he drank all in one gulp again and gave him the horn. He had had enough for that day.

"She will make a good wife. Her parents are respectable people. Her father is my friend, only that he feared to go to war. We have known each other for a very long time. And you say you have not yet met a girl."

Frederick opened his mouth to speak, shook his head and then remained silent again. The old man had been looking at him very keenly.

"What is it my son? You seem to be worrying yourself far too much over matters you should dismiss and go over to more important things. What is it? Talk to me. What I have said, does it offend you?"

"No, father. It doesn't."

"Then what? You don't like her?"

"I like her."

"Then what is the matter? I hate to see you so troubled."

Frederick tightened his lips, plucked up courage and told him:

"That girl won't marry me."

"She said so?"

Frederick nodded but without opening his mouth.

"She is sick in the head," Chief Mutare cursed. "With the mouth of a pig that every member of that family has, I did not know that she would behave like the pig itself. Put food in the plate for a pig, it will first drag it to the ground and mix it with mud and dust before eating. Let her die there. She is just resembling her mother. Her mother was a witch, a real witch. Did you say you asked her and she refused?"

"She refused, father."

"And did you not tell her why you wanted to marry her?"

"I did, father. Everything."

"And she still refused! I can swear in the name of all the gods that that girl has something to hide. She is not normal, she has a problem which she is afraid will be discovered. Yes, that is the truth. I have been wondering why a girl of that age should still be alone. People who know her cannot waste their time asking her. If you asked me before going I would have warned you not to pass there. She is the kind of girl who can bring bad luck to a family if you see them early in the morning." He spat a large glob of mucus on the floor in front of him which he stood up and rubbed off with the sole of his left foot.

"Let her refuse, empty gallon. I know that his toothless father must be behind this refusal. Don't go there again. We will give you a wife this very night and we will march you and the girl in front of their house tomorrow morning. You hear me?"

Frederick smacked his lips but did not say anything.

"She thinks that without her you cannot be Director. She is too small. I can't even sniff her…"

'And even if I am not made Director, what is that to me? I am a qualified medical officer…"

"There is no such thing as IF. The job is ours and we will take it. You have done your part, leave the rest to me." So saying he fumbled into his raffia bag for his snuffbox which he held in his left hand, struck the cover of the snuffbox with his right thumb and recited a few words inaudibly: "I go by land I come by sea. Whatever is mine remains mine. I ask only for that which belongs to me by right."

Frederick looked on, confused. He knew that although he had told his father that the interview was not to be made known to the public, he knew that so long as his father knew it, it won't be a secret for long. And yet, it was suicide for him not to tell him! But there was in the piece of news itself some complication. Because of the problem created by Beatrice's refusal, you could not proceed without letting the cat out of the bag. He noticed how angry his father was and was even more disturbed that he was the object of the anger although he honestly did not know how he had offended the old man.

Chief Mutare was especially angered by his son's nonchalance vis-à-vis the office of Director. After a few pinches he put the snuffbox back in his bag and sat back until he felt his nerves calming down. Then he began again:

"My son, is it that you do not know what honour this office of Director brings to me personally as your father and for your tribe as a suffering people or what?"

Frederick remained silent.

"Do you know that the post of Director is like Minister?'

"Well, well…"

"Do you know that it is the Director who chooses those to enter the nursing colleges?"

"Somehow he is part…"

"Do you know that it is the Director who tells the Minister who to take into the Medical School and who to leave out?"

"Well, I know that…"

"You know that our people have only two nurses in the government services? The rest are from small private, unapproved medical institutes."

"I didn't know that."

"Then know it from today. If I reasoned like you, people would forgive me because I have the excuse of age and alcohol which dulls my brain. What excuse do you have for reasoning like a woman whose husband has died? All these things that I am saying, do they mean anything to you?"

"Father, they do."

"If they do, Frederick, if they mean anything to you, don't put us to shame."

Frederick strained to tell the old man that given the qualification that he had, he could still exert a lot of influence on anybody and cause things to happen to the tribe. But he knew how his father would take it. His mind was focussed only on the title of Director, no less no more. In smouldering anger he left Frederick sitting on the veranda and went out to town.

The old man was visibly angry, but only as angry as a father can be to a child who has erred. They say if a child excreted on your thigh you would clean it, you won't cut off your leg because of that. At thirty-four, Frederick was past the age of flogging, but he was still his child. He must be called to order.

Chapter Nine

Frederick had a lot of respect for his parents and never brought a woman into their family home. Not that his father did not know that he chased women. As a matter of fact, not only did his father turn a blind eye on his relationship with women, but he even encouraged him. On several occasions when he was at home for holidays, his father would invite him out for a drink. He would also ask his friends, Mbe Mimba and Pa Ambrose to join them. At the end of the day when the bill came he directed the bar man to present it to Frederick.

"But it was you who invited me out, father."

"Of course, I know. You mean with you alive I should be wasting my money on bills?"

On one occasion, three ladies came and sat with them one on each side of the old man. Chief Mutare asked Frederick in the vernacular to give them drinks. Frederick looked scandalised and confused that he should give drinks to women who came to sit by his father. As if reading Frederick's mind Chief Mutare cleared the mist:

"So you think these women came for me? The cutting edge of my weapon got blunt years ago. Give them drinks," Chief Mutare urged. "Don't mind that they are sitting with me. They came because of you. Give them drinks even if you do not want them."

To show the extent to which the issue bothered him, Chief Mutare cancelled the Saturday evening cultural manifestations. Nothing stood higher in his mind than giving his son what it took to become the new Director of Medical Services. This was the first time the event was being postponed and the young dancers and drummers felt very disappointed, although they all suspected that there must be a very important reason. There were three persons in Mutare's life who needed to know what was happening with Frederick as soon as possible, Pa Ambrose Motiabong, Mbeh Mimba and Sylvester Akweni, his father in-law, the father of his third wife. Motiabong was the current President of the meeting of their tribesmen in Kumba central, a position which Mutare had held for fifteen years. Mbeh Mimba Thomas was the Treasurer of the group. But his going to see them that night had nothing to do with the meeting. Until the day before, he would have included Emmanuel Afesseh amongst the friends to confide in. But because he was the father of the girl who had disgraced his son in the hope of causing him to lose the office of Director of Medical Services, Afesseh was now his number one enemy, even without knowing that.

They were all good childhood friends who had been separated by the War but had been reunited around the 1950s as young men. They had married within the same decade, but Ambrose Motiabong was the last to get married. His eldest child, a girl was only sixteen. After giving birth to four children, his wife died at childbirth. Motiabong was a man who thought about the future of his children very carefully and so, even as early as that, was very wary about having too many children. If they all grew up to be intelligent and you did not give them the kind of education that they deserved, he thought, you were inviting trouble into the family. Thus, in spite of the loss of his wife he was satisfied with the five children he had to bring up.

But two years after the death of his wife he found the pressure of another wife weighing so heavily on him that he sent word to the village. A young girl of eighteen was brought to him. He was then in his early sixties but extremely virile. But the new wife soon got fed up with him: she had not gone into marriage only to take care of another woman's children when she had a womb to bear her own children. Bibiana, for that was what she was called, noticed that her husband was not treating her own children with enough love and respect, he treated them like accidents of the relationship rather than as God's gifts. After the third child she took off with a young carpenter who used to hover around the Motiabong homestead doing slight repair work.

With the young carpenter, Bibiana's own philosophy caught up with her. Having had two more children with him, she was beginning to feel tired of childbearing. Lissomba Dennis, the carpenter did not see why he should take the risk of seizing somebody's wife only to come and bring up that man's own child. He urged Bibiana to give him two more children at least, which she did. One day, at about noon, a taxi halted at the road side and a small half-clad girl of about three hopped out of it with a parcel wrapped in black plastic paper. An adult female spoke to her from the back seat of the taxi and pointed to the people sitting on the veranda. They were Chief Mutare, Ambrose Motiabong and a neighbour, they were chewing groundnuts and conversing. The people watched the drama from where they sat because Motiabong's house bordered the highway. The little girl darted across the muddy yard into the veranda.

Motiabong who had been studying the little stranger keenly immediately recognised her as his daughter with whom Bibiana had absconded.

"Helen!" he shouted.

"Papa," the little girl answered.

'Wusai mamy?"

"Mamy dong go."

"Dong go fo wusai?" Mutare asked.

"Fo has," she said.

"House dey fo wusai?"

"I no know," she said."

The adult female in the back seat who did the pointing was most probably her mother, Bibiana.

Ambrose Motiabong listened to Chief Mutare's recital very carefully and with a lot of sympathy.

"I don't know why God put all of a woman's intelligence only between her legs," he wondered when Mutare mentioned that Beatrice still refused to marry Frederick even when she knew that the very important post of Director awaited him. Then striking an attitude of regret he pulled at his lower lip for a while, shaking his head.

"Anything the matter?" Mutare enquired.

"Nothing. I am only wondering why I could not have an older girl. My daughter is only sixteen years old. But you know that women are like mushrooms. They bloom in the morning and by evening they wither unrecognisably. You may be thinking that she is a child now, give her two years in a marital home and you will call her a mother."

Mutare tried to consider that possibility. He would consider any possibility that would give his son the job.

"What happens to her school?"

"Ah ah! Do we not send women to school only to help them get better husbands? If a good husband shows up now what good is school anymore?"

"It looks like my son even considered that possibility too. But the lady he really had in mind is Mbe Mimba's daughter. In fact, when I was telling you this story it was she that I was thinking about."

"So we go there in the morning or how, my first man?" Motiabong asked.

"If it were an affair for the morning why then did I come to remove sleep from your eyes? Tomorrow is meeting day. We should straighten everything out before meeting so that by the time we meet there should be no worriness in our hearts. We go there, even if they are asleep we get them up. Who would not surrender his daughter if the only thing he has to lose is a few hours of sleep?"

It was past nine when the two men arrived Mimba's residence, a distance of close to two kilometres down Fiango, which they did on foot. There was total darkness in the Mimba compound, a sign that they were already asleep. When he knocked and flashed his light Mbe Mimba himself got up and enquired from within:

"Who be that?"

"You want me to be shouting my title in the dead of night like this?" Mutare asked.

"It is Chief Mutare," Ambrose Motiabong announced as though he himself were of no real consequence. There was trepidation in the man's voice as he fumbled with the lock and then the bolts and finally opened the door.

The man recognised the voice. "What is the matter, my brothers?" he asked immediately. "You alarm me a great deal."

"Nothing to fear," Mutare said. "I just want us to talk. It's not a death or anything like that. But it is something that can cause death if it is not well handled."

Physically a very frail man, unlike Chief Mutare, Mbe Mimba was a man with perennial health problems. He was a prey to frequent attacks of arthritis and gout which had completely deformed him: his knees, elbows, ankles and the knuckles of his fingers were covered with pronounced bulges, which, as he said, ached more than labour pains. Moreover, he lost his left arm and left eye in a lorry accident that almost took his life many years ago. He now wore and had since worn an artificial hand which he screwed into a device fitted to his shoulder whenever he travelled and wanted to conceal the defect. This made life all the more difficult for him.

It was no surprise, therefore, that it took him about ten long minutes to crawl out of bed and open the door wider to permit them to enter the house. He was without his artificial hand, but he was carrying in his right armpit the Loans Register of the meeting. He was sure that the two men were coming to borrow money, one of them coming to surety the other. He was also carrying a kerosene lamp.

"You sleep so early, my brother?" asked Chief Mutare. "You must be feeling fine."

"Not actually sleeping," the man said groaning in pain. "Low current, the lights kept going out and returning, going out and returning. We just decided to put the whole nonsense off and go to sleep."

"If there was a way," Mutare suggested, "we could talk at the veranda here, let's not disturb the children."

The man kept goats and chickens as a hobby. In the night the goats sleptat the veranda. They had been there when the visitors came but they scampered away in fright. The veranda was littered with goat droppings. Mbe Mimba woke up his son and asked him to clean the place and put some chairs there for them.

"These goats have turned the veranda into their hotel and latrine," the man said. The young man promptly obeyed and it was just as well he did because all through the conversation the visitors kept sniffing uncomfortably. Noticing the discomfort of his friends Mimba apologised for the smell.

"Never mind," Mutare said, "we are not sleeping on it. When the chairs were assembled Chief Mutare went straight to the point:

"Mbe Mimba, is your daughter married?" He spoke in a low voice glancing over his shoulder at the door way.

Mbe Mimba had not sufficiently shaken off the slumber and he had still been thinking of the purpose of the mission when the question was asked. What did the question imply? Had his daughter snatched another woman's husband again as it was reported some time ago? Was she pregnant?

"What is the matter?"

It was Ambrose Motiabang who spoke this time:

"Chief means to ask you whether you have already found a husband for your daughter."

Mbe Mimba had two wives, Waburga and Anastasia, about whom there was an intriguing story. When he married Anastasia, the beautiful daughter of a neighbour and kinsman, Kimu Manfred, for twelve years the woman remained childless. All effort to give her a child were fruitless, medicine men turned his house into a farm: every week they brought fresh herbs which they sold to the man. Some would assure him of instant pregnancy, take large sums of money from him, go and, as they put it, "work the woman" for a week in their laboratory and then return her completely used up to her exasperated husband.

In the midst of mounting pressure from his family he took on Waburga as a second wife. As fate would have it Anastasia mysteriously regained her fertility and became pregnant almost at the same time as her mate. The two ladies gave birth to two boys and thereafter it became a competition and in the end the man who would have been satisfied with three children had thirteen children, eight boys and five girls. Anastasia's first daughter and Mbe Mimba's oldest girl child was Rosita who was in her twenty-fourth year. When Chief Mutare put the question, it was understood that he was referring to the girl.

It took him quite a while to come fully to himself and to recall that Chief Mutare had a son, Dr. Frederick, who was unmarried and could have sent his father to go wife hunting, a very welcome idea. This realisation struck him with instant excitement and he rose and went into his cellar and returned with a four-litre bottle of red wine, "Manjonga" which he set in front of his prospective father in-law. He went back into the house, the visitors thinking that he was going to bring something to add to the wine. It was quite late, but none of them protested. Chief Mutare had long taken his drinking horn from his bag and was whipping it clean and dry in readiness.

Mbe Mimba returned with his daughter sleepwalking and dangling behind him. She was wearing a velvety nightgown with long sleeves which covered her fingers. The gown was so long and big that she held it up like a bride's wedding garment. Apparently Mbe Mimba had whispered something into her ears because even though she still looked sleepy, there was some excitement about her that seemed to have been just switched on.

"Rosita, greet these strangers and get us drinking glasses for this mimbo," he ordered.

"Yes, papa." She went in as Mutare and Motiabong exchanged meaningful glances. When she came she opened the wine and served them, beginning with Mutare. As soon as she finished and looked like withdrawing, Mutare enquired superfluously:

"Do you know me?"

"Yes, papa. I know you very well. You are Chief Mutare. You are doctor's father."

Mutare smiled a knowing smile and muttered:

"Very good at all."

"That's how she is," Mbe Mimba remarked. "Every inch a woman. Wake her up at any hour of the night, she is still the mother of the house. Rosita, my daughter is not married, if that is what you want to know, Chief."

At this point one of his wives opened the door, lowered her head into the veranda and greeted timidly. Apparently Rosita had whispered something to her too. Mbe Mimba waved to her to leave them.

"No, let her join us," Mutare said. "It concerns her too," he urged. She went in and brought a cane chair which she placed very near the husband, between him and Chief Mutare. "We are here to talk about marriage, my wife" the Chief continued. "We want to know whether your daughter Rose is married."

"She is not married, Chief, although she has reached womanhood and will soon be passing."

"They have asked you a simple question," the husband stepped in nudging her. "Answer yes or no. You begin to tell a history."

"She is not married, Chief," she repeated.

"Yes, my friend had just confirmed before you came in. This is a secret and I know that you are people who keep secrets…"

"Trust us," Mbe Mimba admitted.

"The government is about to make my son the Director of Medical Services. I don't want him to go there before looking for a wife, he would never find the right one. I want to give him a wife before he takes up the job. That's why I asked whether Rose was married or not because my son and I have talked about her for some time now."

The woman changed the position of her legs, sat up and enquired worriedly:

"But, Chief, what of my Mbanya Rufina's daughter, Mr. Afesseh's daughter. I thought I heard somebody saying that it looks like something was happening between the doctor and the girl?"

"Prrrahahhh!" the man spat contemptuously, cleared his throat and threw a glob of mucus into the darkness engulfing them in the veranda. "Those are stories," he said cocksurely, "my son only marries the woman I choose for him. Her father is a Catechist, and I don't like them."

The woman shrugged and said for the third time:

"Our daughter is not married."

Chief Mutare asked to talk to her alone. When she came her parents left her with Chief Mutare and his friend in the veranda and went in. Chief Mutare did all the talking and when it came to Rosita's turn she said:

"Chief, I do not have any objection to it all since you are saying it in the presence of my parents too. Only that it would have been better for doctor himself to say these things to me himself."

"My children obey me. I am their eyes, I am their ears, and they believe in my judgment. What is good for me is what is good for them. I will arrange for him to meet you and talk to you at the meeting tomorrow."

And there the mission ended. All the parties involved looked satisfied. Chief Mutare was happy that he had secured his son's job by getting him a wife. Ambrose Motibo, his good friend was happy that he was part of the exercise, and the Mimbas were happy that their daughter had finally found a well-placed husband.

But Chief Mutare had fears which he did not disclose to his kinsmen. Madam Anastasia was a very polite woman, very beautiful and a very good cook. But, having lived with them for so many years, he knew that the woman was not very blessed with natural intelligence. On several occasions he had been in Mbe Mimba's company when the latter had insulted the woman's stupidity. She would make a market list, forget it at home and return with items that were never included in the list. She would prepare soup and forget such an important ingredient as salt. Mbe Mimba often blamed her for the poor performance of their children in school. He said they were taking after their mother.

One day, without knowing that they would be in-laws Chief Mutare shouted at her when they came home and found Anastasia holding her baby upside down, throwing her up and catching repeatedly. At first they thought she was just exercising the bones of the child. But when she continued vigorously Mutare asked why she was doing it.

"I have just given him medicine," she said. "I was supposed to shake the bottle well before giving him, but I forgot. I want the medicine to mix."

Chief Mutare was a very superstitious and suspicious man. He knew of the numerous incidents of dullness and bareness and feared, though remotely, that these infirmities could be visited on her daughter and thus give his son defective offspring. He therefore decided to make another try. Another family from which he thought a suitable wife could come for his son was that of Stanislaus, a former headmaster. He was a domineering personality who had three daughters, all of them in colleges and very near marriageable ages. He had a lot of influence over his children although he was a far cry from the domestic tyrant that Mutare himself was. He decided that it was too late for him to bother his father in-law, Sylvester Akweni.

Early on Sunday morning he paid a visit to the Headmaster, alone this time. He told the now familiar story. It was something to consider, Stanislaus said. But he wasn't ready to interrupt his daughter's education because of marriage, no matter how attractive it sounded. He told Mutare that he didn't think his son would be interested in a girl who still had at least two years to go in college.

"These two years you are talking about is just about fifteen months. My son wouldn't mind. The reason I have cared to come is because he has indicated that he himself needs some years to settle down. The important thing for now is for him to have an official document. The rest will take care of itself."

The idea was finally attractive to Stanislaus and he promised to come to the meeting with his eldest daughter, Emerencia. But he would not permit Chief Mutare to speak to her alone as he had wanted.

Chapter Ten

Chief Mutare arrived his home at midnight, just thirty minutes after Frederick had returned from the Club. He went straight to his own apartment and spoke to him: "where have you been all evening?" he asked.

"I just thought I should relax a bit in the Club, father. I have been under tension the whole day. It's unhealthy."

This was not what he expected to hear.

"You are relaxing in the heat of battle, my son?" He expected Frederick to tell him of the efforts he had made since they parted towards the acquisition of the Directorship. He did not tell Frederick how much groundwork he had done. He was proud of his achievements which he was determined to impose on his son.

"Where is the battle, father? Why try to make mountains out of mole hills? Why create a problem where there is none? I thought I told you that I would solve that problem my own way…"

"That your own way will lead nowhere."

Although he had solved the problem for his son more or less, he did not like the way he was responding to the situation. He decided to give Frederick something to think about overnight, a foretaste of the job he had done while his son was relaxing.

"Do you know Rosita Mimba, my son?" he asked abruptly.

"Rosita Mimba, Rosita Mimba," Frederick repeated the name to himself as he tried to reflect. In the end he confessed: "The name doesn't quite ring a bell. But If I see her I might know. What about her?"

"I want you to know her very well because that girl is very ripe for you. Tomorrow morning we will go and visit them so that you get to know her."

Frederick yawned tiredly and stretched himself, indicating that his father was disturbing his sleep. "Perhaps she is ripe, father, I have no way of knowing. I have said I do not know her." He did not really know her. "And it is not correct for me to go there only to know her. I cannot get to know her for the first time in her father's house."

"We are your eyes, we are your ears. Trust us, trust what we see and tell you or what we hear and tell you. Are you saying that I should arrange for her to come here so that you know her well well?"

"I have not said so either. Since we are not sure of anything, we cannot raise anybody's hopes by creating the impression that I am interested in her. I may not. Let a situation just arise in which I get to see her and know her without alerting her to any hidden intentions."

"Then you create such a situation…"

"I don't need to create it, father. Such situations exist. Look at the family meeting like tomorrow, sons and daughters attend. That is a forum for me to see her and know her."

"Will you be able to talk to her at the meeting?"

"I do not need to talk to her, father. The point is that I do not even know her. I have never seen her. I just want to see her. Thereafter anything can happen. Who knows? She may be the kind of girl I really need. She may be just another girl."

Chief Mutare interpreted this to mean that Rosita had been invited by her son to meet him at the meeting the next day. What the old man did not know was the fact that in his mind Frederick was not thinking of the office of Director. He was not thinking of another woman to discuss marriage with. He was thinking only of reconquering Beatrice. He was sure that he would lose the job of Director of Medical Services, but that was the least of his worries. If he lost that office and won a woman of the calibre of Beatrice who cared for her personal honour more than an office, then it was not a bad bargain. There were not many women who would reason that way. And that was his kind of reasoning. The office itself was immaterial. He would make no more effort to get married so that the Commission would have a good reason to reject him. And then he would go back to Beatrice after that and put his proposal again. Besides, he may even go private. He would set up a private practice, his long-cherished desire since his Edinburgh days. That would allow him more than enough time to carry out his research. He would find out what it takes to set up a research centre. He would write to his friends, acquaintances and well-wishers abroad and ask for assistance in realising the project, if the situation arose.

Chapter Eleven

Frederick's junior sisters took turns in cleaning his room, getting warm water for him to bathe and preparing breakfast for him. That Sunday it was Ruffina's turn. She was eighteen, getting to nineteen and Frederick thought she might be of help in identifying some of the girls his father was talking about. He waited until she had finished dusting the room and was about to shut the door and continue with the parlour, then he asked her:

"Papa was talking to me about a certain girl last night whom he thought I knew or ought to know or should try to know, but whom I really don't know. You know when Pa talks, he does not give you room for any contrary opinion."

"Who is she? What's her name?"

"The name is Rosita, the daughter of Mbe Mimba…"

"I know her very well, brother. I went to school with her, we play in the same handball team. We even attend evening classes together."

"Try to describe her to me. Imagine that somebody has given me a letter to deliver to her and I have come where she is standing with many other girls, describe her to me so that I can go straight to her and give the letter without asking anybody else for help."

That was a tough one! Ruffina pulled a chair from the dining table and went and sat at the door between Frederick's sleeping room and the parlour. She put her left index finger between her teeth and searched her mind for a few minutes for the appropriate words: In height she was only slightly shorter than Fred, though more plump and a bit muscular on account of her indulgence in sports. Her mother was a very big woman, really big, and so also was her father. She took after them in stature.

She had long hands and fleshy calves. She was naturally light in complexion but may appear even lighter now because of the types of creams she uses. Her breasts were large although they did not affect her performance in the games she played. Her buttocks were rather thin and far less pronounced than her breasts. She was very agile for her size. She had very long hair which she nearly always parted in the middle, plaiting the two bunches into long locks that reached down on her shoulders. Very sociable and humorous, always had an interesting story to tell about any occasion. Over all, she was a very nice girl. Very caring and obedient, she always goes to the farm with her mother every Saturday.

Intellectually she was not very sharp. Two of her junior ones were already in the university where she ought to have been two years ago. She was still struggling with the G.C.E. Upon graduation from Queen's College she had four papers at the Ordinary Level – History, Geography, English Literature and Religious Knowledge. This was not considered a pass. Four papers including Religious Knowledge was no pass, especially if it excluded English Language. She needed to have passed in four subjects at least, including English Language and excluding Religious Knowledge. One year after graduation she registered for five subjects including English Language. She passed in English Language but had only two others including religious knowledge. This year in the evening classes she had decided to enter for the Advanced Level in History and Literature while repeating the entire Ordinary Level examination, a monumental task. But he could always educate his wife the way he wanted, Ruffina thought.

"Do you have a picture of her somewhere I can see?" Fred asked. "I don't want to go to the meeting only to see her as Pa was saying."

"I have many pictures in which she figures," Ruffina told him and immediately hurried out. She soon returned with three pictures. In one Rosita stood with Ruffina and another girl, they were all simply dressed with their upper bodies exposed. Frederick nodded at the bulbous breasts his sister was referring to. They were really heavy. Too heavy for his liking. She had a big upper body which grew thinner as you descended until you got to her legs which were like tiny pegs. The second picture concealed her entire bust and arms behind a sumptuous traditional wear. The long hair was very pronounced. The third picture was that of their handball team. She had heavy thighs and calves and was wearing kneecaps which aggravated the thickness of the thighs. Those tiny peg-like feet again!

She was not good enough, Frederick resolved. She did not match the beauty of Beatrice from any angle. She may never make it intellectually, he concluded. He wanted a ready-made girl, not a girl he would worry about educating. Her dullness might neutralise his intelligence and produce an intellectually defective child. He would not even attend the meeting, his mind was made up against her and against any other girl that may be proposed. To hell with the office of Director.

"If somebody asked you to look for a girl for me would you choose Rosita?" Frederick asked the sister.

She did not answer immediately. She thought for a while and then shrugged:

"The girl I choose for you may not be the kind of girl you would want. I think there are things men look for in girls which we ourselves do not see. If you ask me to bring her to you I will do so."

"I think your answer is 'no'. You know that she is not good enough for me. And I think so too. I will wait."

That same morning too, Rosita had sent somebody to ask if Beatrice could help style her hair for her after mass. Beatrice had agreed to help her friend. Her main purpose for going there, however, was to find out the extent to which Beatrice and Frederick had gone. Beatrice had remained characteristically tight-lipped about the relationship all along. If Frederick had finally decided to go in for her, who was she to refuse? It wasn't her fault and Beatrice wouldn't blame her for snatching her husband. It was a common phenomenon: men falling in love with and even getting married to friends or relatives of their longstanding fiancées. But just to keep her conscience clear, as Beatrice worked on her hair she asked rather disinterestedly:

"Bo, what has happened to Fred? I have not been seeing him much. Or is it because I have not been available myself? How are you people getting on?"

"That your doctor man, he is not serious. As slippery as a mud fish. You just can't understand him, and he makes no effort to understand individual differences. I have just allowed the matter to cool off for some time. Perhaps I approached it too hotly. I have told him to let me rest my head for some time. I would rather not be talking about something that hurts me, let's talk about something else…"

"I am sorry. I didn't mean to offend you. I don't even know what made me think of him now."

They talked about something else, many other things, but Rosita was happy because she had had what she wanted: her friend's relationship with Frederick was waning and if she had been approached to replace Beatrice, then it was a good catch.

Even after receiving the promise from Stanislaus that he would be at the meeting with his eldest daughter, Chief Mutare still had doubts as to the success of his negotiations. Just in case all the other cases failed, he decided that he needed a fallback position. The upshot of this reasoning was that before the family meeting that day he had already made contact with six different families with the offer of marriage on behalf of his illustrious son. Thus at the meeting house that afternoon six girls found themselves together, each concealing her reason for being there, or faking one. Even Aaron Frambu, the caretaker sent his only daughter in for the gamble. The presence of the girls did not in itself constitute a source of concern because the constitution of the clan stated very explicitly that every family was liable to a fine of three crates of beer if it did not encourage any children living with them to attend the meeting every Sunday, particularly those over the age of eighteen. But it was not a hard and fast rule and could not be seriously enforced because many children living with their parents were students and could always hide behind school assignments to avoid attending, could always excuse their absence on the pretext of school assignments or other engagements. It was therefore a bit unusual to see so many girls at the meeting, some of whom had never attended, some of whom were still attending school.

The family meeting place was a large hall, half the size of a tennis court, in a building that contained four self-contained bedrooms which were usually hired to visitors in transit. In this way the meeting saved money on rents and was also able to provide for drinks at every session. Aaron Frambu took care of the building and every other thing relating to it. The place was also furnished with a bar which was frequented mostly by their tribesmen. Its realisation was Chief Mutare's brainchild and it stood as an eloquent testimony of the solidarity of the clan, an inspiration to other tribes that were hitherto contented with renting premises. But, on several occasions it had been abused. An unfortunate incident occurred once when a tribe's woman threatened to burn down the building because she discovered that her husband had been bringing girls there to enjoy himself. An even more embarrassing incident occurred when a tribesman trailed his wife to a room in the building and barricaded her inside with her lover for two days. Other than that, it remained a standing achievement in the public eye.

Each family had come unaware of the fact that it had other competitors to contend with. At first each of the girls inwardly thought it was by sheer coincidence that the others were there. But gradually the truth became known. When the meeting was about to begin they were ushered in and shown a conspicuous place to sit near the front row where the women sat. Gradually the more mature amongst the girls began to feel hurt and embarrassed. They found it too demeaning to sit in there doing nothing, even though it was worth the wait. Almost all of them found this a revolting way of meeting a husband. Almost without exception, they found their pride hurt. Rosita, for instance, who had come with so much excitement and hope after visiting Beatrice, found her spirits completely dampened with the arrival of every new girl. Yet none of them left because their parents kept reassuring them that Fred would come any moment.

While the girls perspired with anticipation and gnashed their teeth with embarrassment, those of them who already knew that Dr. Ngenito was having an affair with Beatrice Afesseh but who had not been thoroughly convinced that the whole thing had flopped, had another worry: they wondered why Dr. Ngenito and Beatrice were absent. Were their parents sufficiently informed about the split between the two? If not, they could very well have been made fools of themselves while the two were somewhere cementing their love relationship.

On her part, Beatrice who had made it a habit of always attending the meetings with her father had decided to be absent on that particular day. She did not know how far the story of her refusal to marry Dr. Ngenito had spread, but she was sure it would not be a secret for long, and did not know how she herself would respond to it if anybody tried to know from her. An even more important reason was that she was sure Dr. Ngenito would attend and she did not know how they would react in each other's presence. She had told her mother of what had happened between Dr. Ngenito and herself. Her mother loved and respected her daughter very much, but she made it clear that her daughter had made a big mistake, and she had reacted the way any concerned mother would react: she had reprimanded her for throwing away a God-sent opportunity.

"Next time you are faced with a situation like that," she advised her daughter, "ask the man to give you time, even twenty-four hours, to think about it. During that time you can sound the opinion of other people, friends or relatives, so that when you give an answer at last you know that it is just the kind of answer that any other person in your shoes would have given, the kind of answer which every reasonable person would have expected you to give." She told her to rethink her decision and possibly call up Dr. Ngenito and talk to him because in such matters no answer is final and it is never too late.

When she told her father later in the night he too was not impressed by her decision and response although he had such confidence in her maturity and judgement that he knew that she must have a good reason for turning down the request. He told her:

"Although I have told you over the years that I wouldn't choose a husband for you, that it is your own personal affairs because in the long run it will be you to live with the man and bear the consequences of your choice, I told you the other time that you are not getting any younger."

A very liberal and God-fearing man by disposition, Pa Afesseh Emmanuel did not really condemn or very much regret her refusal, and did not think it was the end of the world either. He had had such devastating experiences with his two younger daughters that he always thought inwardly that it would be better for a daughter to remain unmarried but happy than rush into a marriage that would turn her world upside down. Mr. Emmanuel Afesseh came late to the meeting. It was just as well he did because Chief Mutare who somehow blamed him for his daughter's rejection of his son's hand, had planned to create a scene, anything to disgrace Afesseh! Traditionally, Mr. Afesseh or "Pa Cata" as he was fondly called, led the opening prayers. On this particular occasion Chief Mutare had planned to disrupt the prayer session. Unfortunately for him the Catechist came after someone else had led prayers. Throughout the meeting Chief Mutare kept staring at him with malevolent eyes. He would look at him, clap his hands in wonder and then shake his head. Finally, the Catechist was forced to react:

"Any problem, my brother? Why do you look at me and behave as if I am owing you?"

"You don't know what you have done-eh? That your church that you go every day, you preach one thing and practice the opposite."

"What do you mean, Chief?"

"Order! Order!" the Chief Whip shouted and saved the meeting from degenerating into a brawl for which Mutare was apparently very ready and itchy.

Chief Mutare had come to the meeting knowing that it was going to be a very important day in his life, in the life of his son and in the life of the tribe. He wore a large traditional gown made of dark blue cloth with red and yellow striped cloth strips edging around the neck, it's wide open sleeves and the bottom hem. His son Ben had come with him, carrying his special fly whisk, mat and one of his many traditional bags. The fly whisk was made of yellowish horse tail with a wooden handle in the form of twin figures covered with cloth embroidered with light and dark blue, red, white, translucent green, translucent blue, and translucent yellowish beads, with designs of cowries and blue cylindrical beads on the stomach and back of each figure. The bag, essentially of raffia weave, was covered with patterned European fabric with red fabric fringe on the sides. Its two handles were made of red cloth sewn on the bag in a spiral. It was embroidered on the front with black raffia fibre in lizard or crocodile motif.

Chief Mutare's discomfort in his traditional regalia was observed by everybody and was shared by those parents to whom he had spoken the previous night and even that morning. Every minute he would glance at his watch and look expectantly up the road, the adrenaline rising in his veins like smoke from a campfire. He sweated, cursed, smiled the smile of acute mortification to himself, clasped and unclasped his hands, clenching and unclenching his fists. He scarcely followed the proceedings of the meeting and about a whole hour to the end, his anxiety reached fever pitch and he was compelled to leave. Signalling to his son Ben, to carry his bag and velvet cloth he left the hall without saying a word to anybody. As he went home he expected to meet his son any minute and then return with him to the group and save his face, his mind a maze of crazy thoughts.

All through the night Dr. Frederick Ngenito thought not of the fact that he would lose the office of Director, or worse still, of Beatrice, the lady who was responsible for the loss, or of the need of remedying the situation by finding an appropriate substitute. He reviewed his past and present and prospects for the future as a medical practitioner.

After talking to his sister Ruffina that morning he shut his door and lay in bed thinking of the magnitude of the assignment that lay before him. The first problem to cross his mind was malaria, a killer that claimed the lives of his people and other Africans by thousands every minute. He thought there must be a way down the line of controlling or even eliminating the disease. He did not know of anybody who had thought of eliminating it. He knew that existing drugs only served to reduce the effect of the disease, not the cure. It occurred to him as though in a trance that it was possible to do something about it, something definitive, and this lay with concentrating not on preventing the attack through immunisation but by concentrating on the source of the infection – the anopheles mosquito. It was a scientific fact that the life span of an anopheles mosquito was twenty-four hours; it was a proven scientific fact that one female anopheles mosquito laid at least one thousand eggs which then hatched into other mosquitoes which continued to propagate the spread of the disease. Finally, it was a proven scientific fact that the female mosquito multiplied after mating with the male. It occurred to him that it was possible, or a way could be sought of rendering the female anopheles mosquito unproductive. This was possible by rendering the male unproductive. Since it was not possible to kill all the mosquitoes a way must be sought to ensure the gradual extinction of the brood by producing a substance which would be sprayed in breeding grounds.

It was at this point in his reflections that his good friend, Raymond arrived.

"I am so glad you've come, Ray," he said. I now have an excuse for not going anywhere."

"Were you being forced to go somewhere, doc?"

"My old man left the house insisting that I should join him at the family meeting at Fiango where he planned to introduce me to some girls from which I would choose a wife. Just imagine something like that, Ray!"

"So now you will tell him that I kept you back not so, doc? You know how erratic your old man usually is. Don't let him plunge his dagger into my intestines for nothing sake."

"He can't go that far…"

"I was fearing. By the way, doc, that brings me to the reason for coming here. I have thought about that girl Beatrice's conduct with great bitterness and think that it will be wrong for us to let her get away with it. We must do something to hurt her. The ignominy of her rejection seems too heavy for me to bear with any amount of patience."

"How were you thinking of hurting her, Ray, beat her up or something?"

"Something very mean, as mean as her rejection, came to my mind. We come up with the story that she has been tested positive for HIV/AIDS and we sell the idea to some notorious gossips. She will never find a man to marry her, even if she changed her planet, the scandal would follow her like a shadow."

Fred forced a smile in which contempt was written all over it. Putting his right hand on his friend's left shoulder he said:

"As you have described it so well, that is indeed as *mean* an idea as it possibly can be. But we are not mean people, Ray, remember. We are people of noble upbringing. Even Beatrice herself is not a mean creature. She too is a lady of immense respect. My approach to the problem is different. We have to beat her at her own game without selling ourselves at so low a price."

"And how is that to be done, doc?"

"We should think about reconquering her. In my mind I see myself winning her back and marrying her."

"Jesus Christ of Eborakum!" Raymond exclaimed and looked at his friend with disbelief. "How do you think we can reconquer that girl without belittling ourselves?"

"I will do it and emerge unscathed, my self-esteem undiminished. To sit back bemoaning our fate and acknowledging defeat is to do a disservice to my personal integrity and belittle ourselves. You must wait and see how I go about it. With me, nothing under the sun is impossible. Watch and pray."

"I know that with you there is no such thing as the impossible, which is one reason I will die respecting you. But, your determination to get even with her after all that she has done reminds me of what our people say: 'Do not meddle in an affair between a man and a woman. It is like putting your hand between a tree and its bark.'"

Fred would have said a lot more on the topic and would even have divulged his strategy for reconquering Beatrice. But just then Chief Mutare entered the compound and made straight for Fred's apartment, his face stamped into a mask of fury, foaming at the corners of his mouth, a danger sign to all who knew him. He did not answer Fred's greeting, nor those of Raymond. From his standing position and, shivering with anger, he asked:

"Are you normal, Frederick?"

"Of course I am perfectly normal, father. Why do you say so?"

"Did we not agree that you will be present at the meeting?"

"But what is the problem, father? After you had left I thought over your proposal again and decided that it wouldn't be proper for me to come there for that purpose. I had told you that with time…"

"*Geshundekeit!*" he cursed in German. "You are talking shit. Who are you to decide after I have decided? Now, if you know that you are my first piss, leave that rubbish you are doing and hurry to the meeting house and tell all those girls and their parents whom I spent a sleepless night trying to arrange for you."

"Girls and parents, father?"

"Girls and their parents. Yes. You should hurry there and tell them you are sorry that something kept you behind. I spent all night outside to ensure that you have a wife. Do not disgrace me, you know I hate anything that will bring me shame. Go there right now and choose your wife, they are all waiting."

"Father, I cannot go there, not for that reason. In any case, as you can see, I am guested.'

At that point the old man turned towards Raymond as if noticing him for the first time and said:

"You are definitely comfortable in your job, my son, and also in your family. Why then do you people keep deceiving my own son?"

"How can Chief say that kind of thing? How can I deceive a man of this level? What does it profit me to deceive anybody? At least, not my brother Fred."

"But why don't you advise him? Your friend seems to be all book and very little common sense. I have tried to make him see that life is not lived according to books. It is lived through listening to the voice of wisdom, to the voice of your parents who alone know where beneath the surface of this river of life lie the stones on which to step your feet and cross or ignore it and fall and drown."

"Raymond, my father doesn't believe that there can ever be two sides to any situation..."

"If there are any number of sides," Chief Mutare cut in, "I would be the first to see them, my son. I hate to let somebody make me look like a fool when all I am doing is for his own good!" He turned to Raymond: "Your friend thinks that the office of Director is a meaningless thing..."

"Father, how could I ever have said such a thing?"

"Then why do you ignore the only thing you need to do to secure it?"

"I have ignored nothing. I have simply tried to let you see how ridiculous some of your ideas are and to suggest a better alternative.

"*Geshundekeit! Swartzerhund*t!" the man cursed again.

"I told you before that the Directorship is the least of my worries. Perhaps you thought I was just joking..."

"Do not become Director because of your foolishness and you shall have put the Lemoh-Begoa people one hundred years behind. We had gone very far and just when we were about to catch up with the other tribes of the South West, you are singing a different song. Think about the consequences of what you are about to do. After all the book, it looks like you have to go to school again to learn the good life."

Dr. Ngenito smacked his lips, and looked away from his father who was still standing at the door, fuming with anger. How was he to make the old man reason with him? It wasn't him who was to go to school to learn the good life, it was his father. His father was looking at things too narrowly. His father was thinking only of the honour which went with the office of Director, he was blind to the plight of his people. He was unaware of how many people were dying each day from Malaria, typhoid, T.B., and the like. How was he going to make his father understand that there will be greater honour for the tribe if he came up with a cure for their multifarious ailments? How was he going to tell his father that he alone of all the medical practitioners in the country is carrying out research that would save millions of lives? His father was thinking only of himself, claiming that he was thinking of the good of the tribe. He watched the old man saunter away towards the veranda of the main house.

He had hardly stepped onto the veranda when Ruffina arrived from the meeting. She was accompanied by Rosita. She had not actually attended the meeting but had simply passed there to find out how productive her encounter with her brother had been. But finding that Dr. Ngenito had not come and that Rosita was still waiting, she decided that they should come to their place, just in case her presence might make a difference.

Chief Mutare stood at the steps watching them come towards the house. He was elated. He greeted and embraced Rosita very warmly and regretted his remarks to his son which he now thought were ill-timed. He began to convince himself that even though his son had not been at the meeting, he must have made arrangements for Rosita to meet him at home. His son was, after all, not as stupid as he thought. But he should always make his intentions clear and not allow people to jump to conclusions. He showed them the way to where Fred was, and waited to see the reaction.

On his part, when Fred saw Rosita with Ruffina he concluded it must be part or the continuation of his father's plan to impose a woman on him. He greeted the girl morosely, studied her in one contemptuous look and rose and went across to his room and shut the door, implying that he was not to be disturbed. Rosita went away without their talking to each other, although she spent a very long time talking to his father. Chief Mutare's brief excitement soon turned to gall. And there was more to exasperate him. All this while Raymond stood silent, afraid to be dragged into the Chief's ire.

In keeping with his determination to show the Commission how lightly he took the idea of Director of Medical Services, Frederick decided not to attend the second interview. Since they were already thinking of somebody, probably a North Westerner to fill the vacant position, he thought it would be degrading for him to show up knowing that the all-important condition had not been fulfilled. The night before he wrote a letter explaining why he was absent:

The Chairman,
The Commission for Public Health Interviews
The Provincial Delegation of Public Health
South West Province.

Dear Sir;

ABSENCE FROM SECOND INTERVIEW FOR OFFICE OF DIRECTOR OF MEDICAL SERVICES FOR THE SOUTH WEST PROVINCE

I beg to explain my absence at the above interview. In the first place, I have not been able to meet the very important condition you set for me – producing a legal document by this date to show that I am married. When I assured you that I had a fiancée to whom I could get married at any time, I took too much for granted and when

109

I mentioned that idea to her she rejected it. And because of my newness in the place I have been unable to find another woman who suits my taste.

Secondly, I need a lot of time at my disposal to enable me carry out research projects I began right back at Edinburgh. As Director of Medical Services, I figure that I might not really have the time to realise these projects. I have therefore, decided to go into private practice. For these reasons and with all due respect, I will be absent but do appreciate the fact that you had so much confidence in me to have invited me for the last phase of the interview.

Respectfully yours.

Frederick Ngenito Mutare (M.D. Edinburgh)

Part Two

Chapter Twelve

It did not take long for Chief Mutare to reconcile with his son over the problem of marriage as well as the loss of the office of Director. Working through his three friends, Pa Ambrose, Mbe Mimba and Pa Sylvester Akweni, he succeeded in making the old man see that setting up his hospital and research unit rather than marriage was his first priority. The fact that he had dismissed all the women introduced to him strengthened this view. The old man was made to see that Fred's coldness towards the office of Director was not misdirected but a carefully thought out plan. Anything like the Director would simply derail him and make it impossible for him ever to realize his goals. He was finally made to see that a good well-equipped research unit was not much different from a hospital, and would help his people more than the office of Director in the sense that it would offer employment to young men and women from the tribe.

Raymond gave the idea of a research unit his full approval. But he suggested one thing which eventually proved very beneficial.

"We better apply for Government permission to set up a hospital, not a research unit. A research unit is what it is, a unit, whereas a hospital is the thing, it embodies all or several units. The dossier for a hospital is not much different from that of setting up a research unit, although the hospital is a larger entity. You go through the same trouble. It is like a cow and the leg," he said pithily. "It is like choosing between a cow and the leg of a cow. Rather than choose the leg, you should take the whole cow from which you could carve out so many legs, hands, and so on."

"You have said it all," Fred admitted.

Raymond did more than that, he obtained for his friend written information concerning the application for approval. Three things stood out:

1. Feasibility studies by a team from the Ministry of Health

2. The availability of Funds and guarantee of availability of funds to pay staff salaries for three years.

3. The technical staff with which the hospital would take off; the C.V. of three other doctors and ten staff nurses;

"I will take care of the feasibility studies team,once you have a site ready."

As he had suspected, the team included only two persons from the Ministry of Health. The three other members were the Commissioner of Special Branch of the Police, the Government Delegate of K-Town Urban Council and the Senior District Officer, all of whom were very easily bribed into signing and approving of a site they had not even visited.

Acquiring the site itself was no problem. Through his brother Bernard, Fred got to know that his father had a large piece of land in Konye which he could be persuaded to give up as his own contribution to the realisation of the project. Chief Mutare gladly acquiesced to the demand, now that there were no more hard feelings between him and his son. He gave Fred one of his five Land Certificates with which he was able to obtain a loan of fifty million francs to finance the project. In spite of his crudities, Chief Mutare was an extremely astute man and, knowing that they were strangers in K-Town, made sure that he established legal documents for every piece of landed property that he owned.

The file was now complete and forwarded to the Ministry of Health. Chief Mutare and Raymond showed Fred the ropes and he was able to accelerate the process of approval in the ministry. In one month Dr. Frederick Ngenito Mutare was officially authorized to set up and operate a full-fledged hospital in Konye. The name of the hospital which had been coined by Chief Mutare in reminiscence of his small dispensary in the palace was: MUTARE HOPE RISING CLINIC. Work was begun on the site immediately and contractors laboured feverishly to realise the project in good time. Chief Mutare who spent more time at the site than even Fred, was like a watchdog over the materials that were supplied for the construction. He made sure that not a pin was misdirected, misused or stolen as the habit was with builders. He carefully collected all the empty cement bags which he made sure were of the same make. Early in his supervisory activities he discovered that the builders had stolen six bags of cement and then smuggled empty bags of another kind of cement into the lot. The culprits were promptly sacked and thereafter, they suffered no further losses. The builders were genuinely scared of him because he was not above using his fist or his sword on anybody who tried to sabotage the work through any acts of misconduct. During his leisure he tried to give Fred some ideas on how to run a clinic which he thankfully accepted, but knowing he would never use them because they were too outmoded for the kind of thing he was trying to set up.

While this was going on, Fred kept in touch with his former mates in Edinburgh and elsewhere. Mid way through his studies in Edinburgh, he had flirted with the idea of setting up a private research unit some day. In those days he discussed it with many of his pals. The idea became so serious that towards the final years he assigned a good number of his mates the task of contacting various donor organisations which could help finance such a project. Now was the time to renew those contacts.

In the letter of application he had mentioned only the microscopes, reagents and x-ray machines he had, he had not said he was counting on donor organisations. Two of his mates had actually kept up correspondences with donor organisations down to the moment he was writing to them. One of the gentlemen, Bloomsby Bright, was right then in touch with Friends of Africa, a Canadian philanthropic organisation that supplied drugs and other hospital equipment such as beds, wheel chairs, stretchers, blankets and the like, to needy hospitals in various parts of Africa. Although it was religious in origin, Friends of Africa had the strong backing of the Canadian army and Air force which usually assisted them in delivering their needs to Africa. Even before the buildings were complete Friends of Africa supplied one hundred beds, six wheel chairs, thirteen stretchers and bundles of blankets and foam mattresses.

From another source discovered by Nick Dowden, another classmate with whom he had kept up correspondence, he received one more x-ray machine and two ecography machines, an operating table and packages of surgical instruments. They were to send two experts to help set up the equipment when the moment arrived and three volunteer medical officers to help Fred run the place successfully. On paper, therefore, THE MUTARE HOPE RISING CLINIC seemed to be the best equipped hospital in the country. And it continued to receive more and more assistance from abroad in cash and kind. Fred was able to buy a car without any difficulty. It was actually a long wheelbase Land Rover.

The hospital contained a senior staff quarters for Fred and the other doctors, a junior staff quarters for at least twenty-five nurses, six consultation rooms, a dental department and an eye department, a maternity, labour room and an incubator, five laboratories, each with two microscopes and an ample supply of reagents, a workers' canteen and four wards each containing no fewer than fifty beds – one male, one female - one for children and one divided into self-contained compartments for V.I.Ps and senior civil servants. There was a well-stocked pharmacy and for the first year the drugs were to be sold at giveaway prices. When the hospital was complete it was inaugurated by the Minister of Health who hailed it in his speech as the best thing that had ever happened in the private sector of the Ministry of Health. Chief Mutare stole the show with his dress. He wore a specially woven cap with tassels to which tiny bells had been strung so that there was a ringing sound each time he turned his head, and he did it often. There was an enlarged picture of himself in the war front in Burma which one of his wives carried. There was another in which he was receiving a salute with about eight medals on his chest, many of which he bought in the market and hung them. It was almost as if it was he who was to run the hospital. He even suggested that the statue of himself which stood in his palace be moved and put up in front of the hospital. But the idea was promptly abandoned when he noticed that nobody seemed to support him.

Chapter Thirteen

Fred plunged into the affairs of the hospital with frightening ardour. Although he had always believed in discharging his duties wholeheartedly, irrespective of where he was working, the fact that this was his hospital, his personal property, added more impetus to his natural propensity for hard, relentless work. He had recruited two more doctors, young graduates from the National School of Health Science, to add to the three volunteers, every single one of them sworn to make the clinic unique in its success in handling patients. The three volunteers worked cheerfully and tirelessly, but they were easily outdone by Fred. They could not match his breathless pace. They advised him to slow down, to take it easy, to pace himself. But the more they spoke to him, the more involved he got into his responsibilities. He really had no special responsibilities. Whatever any doctor or nurse did was his responsibility. Not that he was meddlesome, but he believed in cross-checking prescriptions, treatments, operations and the like, just so that no error on the part of any of his staff may tarnish the reputation of the hospital which rose to the skies within a few months of its existence. When a doctor had a difficult case in the theatre he made sure he hung around and gave advice where necessary. On his part, he carried out five delicate surgeries a day, in addition to his administrative duties, in addition to making his rounds in all the wards.

The fear of letting down his donor friends forced him to be always alert, it goaded him into redoubling his efforts and energies, advancing still another step higher than expected. The hours of his rounds were seen by many as the high spot of the hospital's day. Nurses on duty, visitors, patients and even the three volunteers, made an admiring procession in his wake. He had a special touch which all patients recognised and appreciated and felt very sad if he passed their beds without touching them. They would smile and chuckle. His jokes to patients were endless, many of them declaring themselves cured even without taking their medications, just from the humour he generated in their presence. For the children to whom he was very specially devoted, he was irresistible: He had a peculiar whistle, to which some of them came to learn to respond, a prearranged signal to warn them that he was approaching their wards and that they should be ready to laugh and giggle. Whenever he picked up a syringe and approached a child he intended to inject, he started by screaming himself and he would do it so seriously that the child would burst out laughing and, before he noticed, he had finished his job and was moving to the next.

Although every doctor was awed by his genius and success, anybody who knew him in his days in Edinburgh would not be surprised. His success at the Mutare Clinic was just a logical continuation of what he had so well begun in Edinburgh. The M.D. programme lasted seven years. Internship started in the third year. Medical students attended lectures two days of the week, including weekends. He first came to the attention of the authorities during his first period of internship. It was at Cowan's Park Hospital, run by Dr. Mike Thompson, an octogenarian racist of the first order whose attitude towards the darker races made Hitler's pronouncements look like child's play. The only difference was that he did not kill, but he did enough damage to a coloured man to have been considered a murderer. All coloured people were specimens for the London zoo and for the laboratory. He never shook hands with a coloured man or creature as he chose to call them, and he never discussed with them, which was rather unfortunate for a medical officer of his status whose reputation in the medical world was legendary, his articles countless.

One day, in Fred's second week, Dr. Thompson hastily, perhaps, diagnosed a case of temporary inflammation of the muscles of the abdomen as strangulated hernia and immediately ordered his three interns who included Fred to prepare the patient for surgery, and went out. When he came back ninety minutes afterwards to carry out the operation, he met the patient sitting outside the theatre with his clothes on. Dr. Thompson felt insulted and when he learned that the "black monkey" had contradicted his orders, he grew furious. He chose to finish with the patient before dealing with Fred who, thinking otherwise had instead prescribed a balm and some antibiotics for the patient.

Bent on proving to the coloured man, the other interns and the nurses in attendance that he was the one who called the shots in that hospital, he repeated his instructions and sat back to watch them carry them out. The patient was prepared and put on the stretcher and taken into the theatre where he immediately set to work. As the coloured man had predicted, the operation was an exercise in futility because it yielded nothing in the form of a strangulated hernia. He cut open the patient's sides at two points as he mumbled to himself, encountering the same result, nil. He spoke to himself at length while the young interns eyed each other with dismay and discomfort.

As a result of his great insight into cases which surprised and embarrassed rather than impressed Dr. Thompson, Fred was sent back to the medical school at Edinburgh as though he had proven to be grossly incompetent, and reassigned to a different hospital. Not all the whites were racists, at least not to the same degree, and the authorities soon found out why Dr. Mike Thompson did not want him and respected him all the more for it. At The Burnley Cottage Hospital where he was reassigned, Fred faired no worse. He continued to see things so differently and correctly that he was permanently assigned to Dr Hart Cromwell, the specialist who handled very complicated and baffling cases. Dr. Hart Cromwell considered him an asset to the profession and made no secret about it. He spoke to Fred very often about medicine and about his future. He gave Fred the addresses of the editors of respectable journals, many of whom he knew personally. The upshot of this relationship was that in his fourth year, the second year of his internship, he wrote two articles:

1. *An Attempt to Obliterate Potent ducts arteriosus in a Patient with Subacute Bacterial endarteritis and*

2. *Combined Ligation of Ductus Arteriosis and Sulphapyridine Therapy in Case of influenzal endateriosis.*

The first was sent to the *Journal of British Medicine* and the second to *Surgery, a Publication of the Medical Faculty of the Massachusetts Institute of Technology, Harvard.*

Both articles were accepted for publication. The Journal of British Medicine sent a copy of his article to Dr. Christian N. Barnard, the South African doctor who carried out the first heart-transplant. The man wrote to Fred and even asked for permission to try his findings on his next patient. Fred was thrilled. He had become an instant celebrity. He was asked to combine the two articles, since they were related and develop them into a book-length study, which he promised to do some day. From the two articles and the fame that came with them he received much financial rewards. The Medical School held a party in his honour and he was awarded a medal of merit. From his articles on Cardiac Surgery, he received in addition to a cash price, ten brand new microscopes, fifty Bunsen burners, slides and packets of reagents. But the high water mark of his career remained the letter from Dr. Christian Barnard.

In his fifth year, however, discovering that cardiac problems were not the most alarming health problems in Africa where he would surely return to, he switched his attention to tropical medicine with focus on malaria and typhoid, T.B and HIV/AIDS. When he wrote to medical institutions which knew his worth and had even published his articles, telling them of his plans to set up a research unit in Africa, and asked for assistance in cash and kind, he was flooded with offers: operating tables, x-ray machines, microscopes, reagents, beds, blankets, medicines and the like.

But Fred was not spoiled by success. He continued to work harder and harder. Three more publications came in rapid succession:

1. An Experimental Method of Providing a Collateral Circulation to the Heart

2. Coronary Sclerosis and Angina Pectoris, Treatment by Grafting a New Blood Supply Upon the Myocardium.

3. Reconstruction of the left Anterior Descending coronary artery; Proximal Vein bypass graft and distal gas endarterectonmy

These articles, published respectively in England, the U.S. and Germany brought him further financial gains. But it was the fame that he enjoyed more than anything else and he was soon reading from such greats as Dr. Grimme Dorset, Professor of Surgery, the University of Birmingham, Queen Elizabeth Hospital; Dr. Hem Griffit Bone, Dr. Arnold Crook, Professor of Surgery, Harvard Medical School, Massachusetts General Hospital, Boston, and Dr. Hermann Britz, Professor and Chairman, Department of Surgery, The Johns Hopkins University School of Medicine, The Johns Hopkins Hospital, Baltimore, Maryland, U.S.A. When he went down to London for a symposium at the Africa Centre, he felt very much flattered by the attention he got from reporters and news photographers.

At his graduation, Professor Ingram Moore, the Dean of the Faculty of Medicine made a comment about him which he always cherished so much. He said:

"We see in this young African doctor the impetus, the determination that led such great names as the Frederick Banting, Charles Best, Louis Pasteur and the Curriers, to make medical history. Without prejudice to his colour, let me tell the world here loud and clear that we have here in the making a black man who will at last bring light to the darkness of the African continent, in so far as the medical profession is concerned. A Nobel Prize in Medicine lies in wait for him."

In this, Professor Moore, a revered scholar in modern medicine in the western world, especially Britain, Canada and the U.S. was a bit inaccurate but this was because his knowledge of Africa was very slim. He knew of Africans mainly from the accounts of David Livingstone, as people who ate ointments prescribed for skin afflictions and swallowed at one gulp bottles of medicine supposed to last weeks.

It was fair, therefore, to say that working hard and breathlessly was a way of life with Fred long before he set up his hospital in the Konye farmlands. He insisted that all members of staff on duty should be at their job sites by eight every morning, but his own ward rounds started well before that. He knew every case in the hospital and knew most patients by name, something that endeared him to the men and women who flocked in to be treated. Patients who could not pay for their treatment were asked to work on the hospital farms in compensation. Sometimes when the people looked very helpless, he simply let them go.

Chapter Fourteen

One night, soon after construction work had been completed and the clinic had been inaugurated, he had a dream: he was strolling along the road one Saturday morning when he suddenly saw Beatrice clad in a wedding dress, clinging to the left hand of a gentleman whose face he could not recognise because he kept turning away from him. All smiles, the two of them were waving to crowds of well

wishers from an open back long Chevrolet which drove slowly by. She seemed to notice Fred in the crowd and he thought she said:

"Fred, good luck with your Directorship. I am in good hands."

They were driving to the City Hall where the reception was. Fred followed them on foot but arrived the gate when the door was shut and the security men could not allow him in because every available space inside had been taken up. Desperate, he took out his business card and wrote on the back of it:

"Madam Beatrice, I came here to wish you well in your marriage, but I arrived when the hall was full and I could not be allowed in. I am still waiting outside the gate, to wish you well." He gave the note to one of the security men who had barred his way and waited. In a minute Beatrice showed up at the gate, frantically looking for him, holding up her wedding garment in both hands, peering through the darkness which had suddenly enfolded the place.

"Are you looking for me, Madam Beatrice?" he shouted from behind the hedge. Just at that time something woke him up. He bit his finger and went back to sleep, glad that it had been only a dream. Yet the thought would not leave his mind. He actually spent the rest of night haunted by the dream and early the following morning he decided to write to Beatrice. He did not mention the dream. He simply said:

My Dear Miss Beatrice;

As you must have learnt so long ago, I lost my job as the prospective Director of Medical Services for the South West Province simply because you would not marry me. To show you how serious I was about getting married to you, I refused to consider any other girl, down to this moment of writing to you. By this I mean to say that I am still unmarried. If you are still unmarried, or unengaged, reconsider this request from the bottom of my heart. I understand you refused my hand the first time on principle, something which is terribly rare amongst young ladies, but which I respected you for, very much. I still love you just as before and I am asking for your hand once more, now that I am not Director of Medical Services.
Stay well,
Someone who loves you.

Fred.

He drove to Raymond's office at Barombi Kang and began with an accusation.

"I have a grudge against you, Ray."

"A grudge, doc? What for?"

"Why have you never asked anything else about my marriage plans since the Beatrice refusal?"

"Heaven is my witness, doc, if that is the grudge you have against me. You must have forgotten that a day after your father confronted me at your place in his house I raised the issue of marriage again."

"What did I say?"

"You said it was either Beatrice or nothing, and that if you would look elsewhere it would take a while and that you would keep me posted."

"It is possible that I said so…"

"You did, doc, you might have forgotten. You know there are so many things in your head. I told you once that you are one of the very few men whose judgement I trust in. I know that before you take a decision or before you say something you must have given it enough thought, such that I find you seldom wrong. I convinced myself that although you were silent, you must be planning something that would impress everybody when it eventually comes out."

"You are right," Fred said with inward pride. 'And listen to this one: I have decided to go back to Beatrice. You know she is still unmarried."

Raymond stared at Fred with malevolent eyes.

"How do you mean?"

"I have given myself these last many months to see if thoughts on her could cross my mind again. They have always done so, and I continue to think of her in very positive terms. I think I still love her well enough to reconsider marrying her."

"That's an interesting one, I tell you. If it were me I would find it very very hard to go back there."

"But it's not you, and I find it *very very* easy to go back. This is the way we are going to proceed…"

"We?"

"Of course you and I. You have a role to play there."

"I am listening."

"I have written a letter for her which I think should put her in the right frame of mind to give me a positive response, unless she is out of brains, which she is not."

"And where do I come in?"

"Since she knows you so well, I would be most grateful if you would take the letter to her and insist on a reply."

Raymond took in a very long breath, pulled down the corners of his mouth and said:

"Thy will be done, doc. I only hope that she doesn't throw a pot of boiling water on me."

They both laughed.

"It wouldn't come to that," Fred said.

Raymond took the letter, weighed it and left. He did not ask Fred about its contents. He simply believed that Fred could not be writing about anything that would embarrass them both. He did not tell Fred that once upon a time he had made a pass at her but had failed. He drove straight to Beatrice's school and called her out and gave her the letter.

Beatrice had long discovered that Raymond and Fred worked very closely together. When she came out of the classroom he said:

"Miss, this letter is for you."

"She took it and held it with a look of some embarrassment on her face.

"What kind of letter is this that it is a big man like you bringing it, sir."

"It is from a bigger man, your fiancée."

"My fiancée? Who is my fiancée, Mr. Raymond?"

"Dr. Ngenito. Fred Ngenito."

She took in a very long breath, held the letter to her chest, looked up into the sky as if imploring the intervention of God and said:

"I will read it later."

"He wants me to bring a reply back, now."

"He again with these his urgent replies?"

They both laughed and then she promised:

"I cannot give you a reply now. I will read the letter later, when you have gone, and then I shall decide when I shall reply. But tell him that I will reply as soon as I read the letter."

"Do I come for the reply then?"

"Do not come for it. I know where your office is."

"Oh, do you?"

"Even if I don't, I shall ask. But rest assured, I shall bring the reply to you."

Raymond relayed everything that transpired when he delivered the letter, Beatrice's reactions, how she looked into the sky and how her heart sank when she learnt that the letter had come from him. He did not tell Fred the fiancée aspect of it.

Fred was satisfied that the letter had been duly delivered and knew that she would reply. The very next day Raymond showed up at the Clinic with the reply. He did not seem anxious to read the contents, but was interested in it. He stood back and folded his hands over his chest and stared down at Fred as he read. Fred's mouth was smiling as he read deeper and deeper until he came to the last line.

"This is as I expected," he said, giving Raymond the letter to read.

Raymond read it quickly but carefully:

Dear Fred;

I received your letter with thanks and a lot of surprise. I could not imagine that you would ever think of me in any positive light after what I did to you. I am not very good in writing letters because, from my own little experience, the written word conveys only messages, it does not convey the real emotion behind the words. Besides, the written word again has the tendency to be misinterpreted. You mean one thing and then the word is interpreted at the other end to mean something else.

What I can suggest here is that you find time and place and let us sit and talk about this issue. It is too serious and important for me to discuss in a few words in a letter. I am at your disposal. Meanwhile, I want to thank you for your compliment on my so-called principles. It looks to me as if you too have the same principles. I usually want to be frank about things that touch me personally, that's why I behaved the way I did. I was actually very sorry afterwards when you left, but there was nothing I could do because it was too late and you had left.

Again, Fred, as I said, let us meet and talk things over. Greet your friend for me.

Most affectionately yours.

Betty.

"Never take women for granted," Raymond said as he folded the letter and gave back to Fred. 'This is a very mature document, brief as it is. I could have sworn that I never associated her with such maturity of thought."

Fred smiled contentedly.

"She is interesting," he said.

"Really interesting," Raymond added. "And the handwriting, did you look at it carefully?"

"Not quite," Fred said stretching out the letter again and nodding. He had not been interested in anything else but the content of the letter, her response.

"So manly. Girls have the tendency of slanting their characters backwards, but see hers, tilted forward and formed like a man's."

"Interesting," Fred said and then went to voice what was uppermost in his mind:

"You know what Ray? We set up an appointment right away. This time I will not write. Tell her that we meet at the Club tomorrow evening at seven. Tell her you will pick her up and meet me there."

"Consider it done, doc. After all, what are friends for?"

On Thursday evening, the day of the appointment, Fred drove to the Club at six o'clock. He knew he was one hour early, but it did not matter. He remembered the old saying: "It was better to be a year too early than a minute too late." He ordered a chicken, potato and plantain chips, and then he sat at the counter drinking his Gold Harp. At a quarter to seven Raymond showed up, but without Beatrice. Fred was alarmed.

"What happened, Ray? She changed her mind?"

"Something of the sort. But she will be here. She changed her mind about coming with me in my car. She said I should just go and that she would join us."

Raymond had hardly finished the last words when in came the guest of honour. Dressed without undue affectation, Beatrice was wearing a grey pullover over a light blue evening dress spotted white and red. She was wearing a dress that reached well below her knees with two tiny blue straps running from the top of the dress just above her breasts, to the back. Her shoes were deep blue, matching the dress, and the heels were moderately high, revealing long toe nails painted pink. She was holding a blue handbag. There was only the faintest makeup on her face, noticeable only if you came very close, slightly pronounced eyebrows and gentle greyish coloration on the lips. Her perfume too had a gentle and sweet odour.

Fred jumped down from the counter, almost missing his step, steadied himself and then stood until she came up to him. He showed his hand which she shook and then, still holding the hand she came close to his body, turned her back and leaned on him.

"Good evening, everyone," she said.

Fred and Raymond greeted at once: "Good evening, Beatrice."

"Let's sit down," Fred suggested and they went into the private room of the Club. There Fred ordered everybody a drink. He told them of the chicken and half way through their drink, the chicken was brought. Raymond washed his hands and tried to cut the chicken up into smaller pieces.

"That's a woman's job," Beatrice said, placed her bag on Fred's laps and pulled the plate of chicken towards her.

131

Very methodically she tore it into bits and then served each person. She put the gizzard in Raymond's plate.

"Why?" Fred asked. "He is much younger than myself."

"He is our guest of honour. Besides, he is your mail man."

They all laughed and fell to chewing and drinking. After his chicken, Raymond took excuse and left to watch television and listen to news. When they had finished eating Fred took a long drink and then sitting up and looking at Beatrice said:

"Betty, welcome again, after such a long time."

"Thank you."

"You suggested that we should rather talk…"

"Did you see my letter, Fred/"

"I saw it, that's why we are here."

"How did you react to it?"

"I liked it. Just like you."

"How?"

"Ruthlessly honest."

"That's me," she smiled. Fred went back to what he was saying:

"So what was it you were afraid to write?"

"I wanted to tell you that I regret what happened very sincerely. I wanted to tell you that I still love you, very much, especially if you are sincere about what you said.

"I mean every word of what I said."

"If so, Fred, take it from my own lips and from my own heart that I accept to marry you."

Fred joined her in her seat and put his right hand over her shoulders. Then they stood up and embraced each other, ending in a very long kiss which was only interrupted by the dragging of feet near the door. They resumed their seats. Fred ordered another drink. He continued to eye her with consummate interest. Her face was flushed from excitement at meeting him again, and had become alive and unusually attractive. Her eyes shone with such radiance that they lit up her entire face, making it all the more beautiful, irresistible. The first impression of unadorned naturalness which the absence of heavy makeup created was accentuated by a pleasing feeling as she threw her hands over Fred's neck.

"This one is a celebration drink, so don't turn it down," he said. He then called for Raymond. When he came in he said:

"Dr. and Mrs. Ngenito invite you to share in their celebration drink."

They all burst out laughing, rose and clicked glasses.

"Congratulations," Raymond said.

"Thank you, Ray. Thank you too for your role in this."

"Fred, let me ask you one thing. I did not want to ask you earlier because it would look like a condition for accepting or refusing."

"What can that be, Betty?"

She took her time, readjusted herself and began:

"Only you know how to handle that your dad. When what happened the last time happened, we heard that he made a lot of noise and threatened to even beat up my father. How do you think he is going to receive this news/"

"You don't bother yourself about my dad. That guy is a phenomenon, but I know how to handle him. We had long reconciled and he is completely on my side. We will explain to him in a manner that would make him less obnoxious to our peace."

"I will be glad."

"I do not see him interfering in my private affairs. After all he has his home and I have mine."

"You are preaching to the converted," Beatrice said.

It was seven o'clock in the morning when Beatrice shook Fred.

"You won't go to work?"

"I have enough doctors to run the hospital," he said. "I am the boss, so don't worry. Let's enjoy ourselves. It doesn't come often."

"That's right," Beatrice said, rubbing him with kisses.

"And you," Fred said. "You won't go to school?"

"I have been so regular that the HM will believe any excuse I give him. You don't know how happy I am being in your arms. God's time is the best, as my father usually says."

With Beatrice assuredly and finally his wife, Fred felt passionate love come over him like a pleasant fever of joy. He had had so many loves in his past life, but never had anyone of them tried his emotions thus far. Beatrice had pushed them to the limits, beyond allowable limits, one would say, the way men in love can only dream. He felt charged, like one who had undergone a kind of baptism or some form of benediction that touched his soul with rapture and belief in the purity of spirit. That feeling of research, that sense of mission through which he had hoped to attain immortality, through which he had hoped to leave his footprints on the sands of time, that permanent and laudable breakthrough in malaria, typhoid, HIV/AIDS and the like, came rushing to his eager brain like fish at the sight of a bait, which needed only lowering and he was a happy man. Love, research, creative research, seemed now to spring from the same source and when he thought of one, he thought of the other.

Beatrice was not so much a wife as a lover who made him see and taste and thirst for love nowhere else. His soul was filled with noble feelings. In his mind's eye he saw himself instantly famous and spoken in the same breath with all the big names in medicine. And in all this, he felt Beatrice leaning over his shoulder and encouraging him like some guardian angel, some spiritual goad. And the very next week he sent off an article that was accepted for publication and acclaimed as record-breaking. He read cuttings of reports on his marvellous research sent in to him by friends abroad, with orgasmic satisfaction. To Beatrice be the glory.

Chapter Fifteen

It took a whole month for anybody outside the close circle of Fred's and Beatrice's friends to know what was happening. Beatrice, however, alarmed her parents by announcing that she was back with Fred and even engaged for marriage.

"Don't let that man go and kill you," her father who was usually reticent on such matters said with great foreboding.

"He will not kill me, Papa, he loves me. He really loves me, I have seen it. We love each other. God will help us."

The old man shrugged and sat quiet. After a while he asked:

"That his tiger of a father, does he know about it?"

"Fred will tell him. He knows how he will tell him so that he does not go about shouting."

Fred, Beatrice and Raymond sat down and set the date for the court marriage and the church wedding and the dimension each would take. He had invitation cards printed and then started working towards the two events. He placed an order for a wedding gown for Beatrice and a cream suit for himself. Then he decided to let his father know about his plans. He did not go to him directly but sought the intervention of Pa Sylvester and Mbe Mimba. The decision to ask Mbe Mimba to intervene on his behalf was a costly mistake because, unknown to Fred, the man had never forgiven him for raising his daughter Rosita high and dry. Mbe Mimba listened to him very carefully and promised to talk to Chief Mutare as a personal friend, to convince him in every way possible, to give his son his blessings in his marriage.

But when he went to Chief Mutare he spoke as though Fred had not come to him, as though he had just discovered a secret which Fred was hiding from everybody else.

"It cannot be," Chief Mutare said. "My son cannot be that mad. Not the woman who made him lose such an important job."

"They are living together already," Mbe Mimba said. "I even thought you were aware of it but were hiding it from me."

"I could not have been aware of such a thing without bringing down the sky," Chief Mutare said. He sent his daughter Ruffina to go to Fred's house at Konye and confirm the rumour.

"It is true, father," she said when she returned. "Brother and Beatrice are living together. She is even pregnant."

That whole day and the whole night, Chief Mutare went about his business like a man possessed. He did not answer any greetings and refused food from his wives. In the afternoon of the next day when he estimated that Fred must have returned from work he told his wives that he was going to chase Beatrice from his son's house.

"If I meet her in that house and my son hesitates to send her back to her father's compound, blood shall spill."

Fred and Beatrice had been sitting on a large armchair, conversing about the day's activities, each telling the other the problems he faced that day and how he overcame them. The arm chair faced the door and so it was possible to see somebody coming towards the house from afar.

"Who is that coming up like my father," Fred said with great surprise. Beatrice rose to the window and as soon as she noticed that he was the one, she escaped into the bedroom, even leaving a shoe behind in her haste to avoid meeting with the old man.

Chief Mutare kicked the door open, entered and without greeting his son asked:

"Ngenito, where is the snake I hear you are harbouring in this house?"

Fred noticed his attire and wondered why the man would be so formally dressed just to come and quarrel. He was wearing a smart outfit of shirt and pants made of red fabric covered with loose netting of bead strand with the neck and sleeve openings decorated with red and blue bead strands, the rest with light and dark blue beads arranged in spear motif. Around the sleeve openings were red cotton yarn tufts and little red cloth pouches. From his side dangled ominously a dagger in a sheath. Fred knew the dagger to have an iron blade that tapered to a point, with the hilt resembling a European sabre and foil hilts. The sheath was made of wood and covered with cloth embroidered with red, light and dark blue beads. There were two handles for fastening the dagger to sash, one on each side. On his head was a cap of indigo blue cotton yarn with cowries and blue cylindrical beads on the front.

Even more surprising was the fact that he had come alone, without Ben. Fred studied him for a brief nervous second and said:

"Pa, welcome, sit down." Fred tried to calm the man down. His breasts rising and falling in anger, the old man refused to sit.

"Pa, why do you continue to treat me like a baby?" Fred asked softly. "I am thirty-eight years old, but that does not mean a thing to you..."

"It doesn't mean a thing to me because you do not behave like thirty-eight years old. You behave like eight years old."

"How do I behave like an eight year old, father? You come into my house by kicking at the door. You do not greet and you do not bother to answer my greetings. And then you think it is me who is behaving like an eight year old."

"I say again, where is that devil?"

"Please, father, if you won't sit, I won't answer any question from you."

The old man literally threw himself into a seat and repeated:

"Where is she?"

"Whom are you talking about? Whom are you calling snake, devil and so on?"

"I mean Afesseh's daughter, whether you call her Beatrice or what. Where is she.?"

"Who said she is here? And what if she is here?"

"If she is here," the old man said, eyeing the ladies shoe Beatrice had left behind.

"If she is here I will tell her what I have in my mind,"

"Which is?"

"Which is that she has no right to be here after what she did to the entire tribe. I do not see how you would ignore all those young girls I campaigned for and cling to a viper. That's the kind of woman who can bring misfortunes into a family."

"Listen, father. Let me tell you that I run my life, myself. I associate with people of my choice, I fall in love with women of my own choice and I bear the consequences, myself alone. If I seek your opinion on these issues it is not because I am helpless, it is out of respect to you as my father. But it doesn't mean that at every pace you will order me around."

For the first time Chief Mutare sensed that his son was slipping away from his rigid control. He braced himself and, leaning forward towards Fred began:

"Ngenito, you fail to see a father's love in all that I do for you."

"I do not, father, don't misunderstand me."

"I am not misunderstanding you. I delivered you, I paid your fees throughout college. I sent you to England. No other child of mine has gone that far. That is love."

"None has merited going anywhere," Fred told him decisively.

"The land on which this hospital stands belongs to me. I gave it to you, free of charge. You were able to be granted loans because of the land certificates which I gave to you. That is love. And, all I ask for in return is a little respect, a little obedience, and you would not give me that."

"I have not denied you obedience, father, I have not denied you respect. You are the one forcing me to disrespect you. You are the one forcing me to disobey you."

"At any rate," Chief Mutare resumed, "I came here for one thing and you have not told me. Is that woman in this house? If she is, my son, do me the favour of sending her away, before my own eyes, before *contry fashn* catches you. When you remained unmarried, we were not bothered."

"But I cannot continue to be unmarried, father. It is time for me to start building up my own family, to start having children. And let me say, father, that that woman you want to send out of this house is several months pregnant."

"Pregnant my anus," the old man cursed. "Are you saying that that was the last drop of sperm in your waist? You can always have children from other women."

"But I have made my choice. She will never leave this house, ever."

"*Geshundekeit!*" the man shouted in his German of the Burma days. "*Swartzerwundt!*" Nobody spoke for close to five minutes. Fred sat back frowning, fuming with anger, waiting for the man to leave so that he would shut his door and go and have a rest. The man sat in his own corner, foaming at the corners of his mouth from sheer anger, bubbles of sweat coursing down his forehead and thickset neck, his breasts rising and falling as he clenched and unclenched his fist, grinding his teeth, biting his lips. Then, rising and casting malevolent eyes on Fred he said almost to himself: "When I allow shit like this to enter my ears as you have been forcing me to do, my bladder gets filled up at once. Please show me where to empty my bowels."

"But you know where to go, father, why are you bothering everybody? Why are you making a nuisance of yourself? Blasius, show pa the way to the toilet."

"I have had enough," the old man said as he followed the boy down the corridor.

Frederick smiled to himself.

"When you have a father like this, you do not need an enemy. He is enemy enough." This last statement was lost in the ominous wind that blew in through the front window and out through the back.

They all heard him key the door when he got in. Ten minutes passed, twenty, thirty, forty, fifty, then one hour, he had still not left the latrine. Fred got a bit worried, not that he suspected or feared anything, he was just disturbed that a man would spend such a long time in the toilet.

"Pa, you want to sleep in the toilet?" he asked half-humorously.

There was no sound. He waited for a minute and then repeated the question. There was still no sound. Anxious, he bent down and peeped into the keyhole. If his father were sitting on the toilet bowl he wouldn't be able to see anything because his large bulk would block his view by cutting off the light and making the inside invisible. He saw through the key hole and could even see the back wall inside. There was no indication that there was anybody inside. He knocked on the door once, then twice and then very violently, there was no response from inside. He shook the handle until it was threatening to detach from the main body. Panic seized him. He called for Blasius and his brother Bernard.

"Do anything to open this door. Pa is not responding, I don't know what he is up to. You know this pa like this, he is such a funny man."

As he spoke he noticed a dark liquid crawling into the white-tiled floor of the corridor from beneath the door of the toilet. He bent down and touched it with his forefinger and examined it in the corridor light. It was crimson red.

"This is blood!" he shouted, moved backward and charged into the door with his left shoulder, injuring it in the process. The upper hinge gave way. His brother and the house boy took over while he stood back with his hands crossed over his heaving chest, knowing something fatal could have happened to his father, although he could not at that time guess what exactly had happened. In a matter of seconds the door was broken and pulled down completely to reveal the soul-destroying sight of his father lying face down across the toilet bowl that was already filled with blood.

Chief Mutare was dead and, quite ominously, he was clasping Beatrice's slipper tightly in his left hand, which he had craftily picked up from the floor after she fled at his arrival. He was a very heavy man, but they managed to turn him over with relative ease, their anxiety lending them unusual strength. He had plunged his sword-like dagger into his chest. His mouth was filled with sawdust which he had swallowed to prevent any sound he made from reaching out. An autopsy would reveal further that he had swallowed a good dose of cyanide before stabbing himself, and that with dead accuracy he had driven the dagger into his heart, through the pulmonary trunk and severing the coronary artery, causing instant death.

Fred sent for his ambulance driver. Meanwhile he tried to pull out the sword and, when he succeeded, blood spurted out in jets all over the toilet, staining the walls. He sent for his first aid box from which he got some plaster and put over the wound to arrest the continuous bleeding. They then carried the man into the ambulance and away to the theatre.

Beatrice remained frozen with fear in her room. When Fred entered to take a bath she did not ask him what was happening because Fred successfully pretended as if there was nothing amiss. After the bath he went to the parlour and opened the cupboard and took out a bottle of whisky from which he took half a glass which he emptied almost in one gulp. Then he told his brother, the ambulance driver and the house boy, the only persons who knew what had happened:

"Listen to me very carefully, all of you. No matter what you know about how pa has died, I want to tell everybody else that he died of a heart attack. Even the fact that we found my wife's shoe in his left hand should also remain a secret. My father has disgraced me terribly."

They all swore that his will shall be done. But Ben had his misgivings.

"Brother," he began, "we shall do exactly as you have said. But, dying like this is a curse. Our people regard it as a curse and the whole house, including its occupants has to be cleansed traditionally. So I don't know."

Frederick reflected for a while, weighing his junior brother's words carefully and then he said: "If they do not know how he died they would not have to cleanse the house, they would not have to cleanse me or us. It will hurt my reputation very very badly if it is known that my father committed suicide in my house. I cannot allow that to happen. Let's keep it as I have decided."

They sat down and drew up a list of the people who were to be informed immediately: Pa Ambrose, Mbe Mimba and Pa Sylvester, the late man's closest friends. It was these three who decided who to be informed and in what order. Then they drove to the theatre. Beatrice saw the ambulance drive off from the bedroom window. She saw that Fred was alone with the driver in front. She could not see Fred's brother, Bernard, who was sitting behind the ambulance with the corpse of his father. To her chagrin, there was no sign of her most dreaded father in-law. All she thought was that there must be an emergency in the hospital requiring Fred's immediate attention, and that he must have left his father waiting in his house. She keyed the door, fearing that the man might want to search the rooms for her presence.

142

Blasius took his time and cleaned the floor and the walls of the toilet. The floor and the walls were covered with white enamel tiles and so it was possible to remove every stain. At the theatre the old man's bloodstained clothes were taken off. Fred's driver was asked to take Bernard back to their compound for him to bring a new set of clothes to put on him. He was also to inform those friends of his father whom they had agreed to reveal the death to first.

By the time he returned to the house Beatrice had fallen deep asleep. He did not wake her up to tell her what had happened. Bernard soon returned with the clothes which he wore on the dead man. He sent back his driver to fetch the old men to whom he described the death by cardiac arrest in the toilet. He took them to the theatre and showed them the corpse and then they drove back to work out what was to be done.

Ignorant that it was a case of suicide, Mbe Mimba told the little committee:

"Doctor seems to be talking of burying his father as soon as possible as if he was an ordinary person. Our late brother was a second class Chief, recognised by everybody, a gazetted chief."

"Of course he was," Fred said without much conviction. "Some chief," he said in his throat. He had never taken his father's chieftaincy seriously. It had always been a big joke to him, although for the old man, it was a question of life and death. "He was a chief," he resumed, "so how do we proceed?"

"We bury him exactly the way all important chiefs are buried. We know you did not believe in him as chief, but the administrative took him seriously and honoured him. He has left behind sons and daughters, a majority of whom took his title seriously and from whom his successor has to come…"

"Count me out of that," Fred interrupted.

"I am still talking, doctor. Even if you are not interested, there are six other brothers who can succeed him."

"Don't get me wrong," Fred tried to correct himself, "I just want to make things easy for everybody. If, for instance, the king-makers knew that there was only one son interested in the succession, they would be glad that they have had their work cut out."

"Nobody is getting doctor wrong. There will be no problem"

Fred breathed in and out nervously, he was a man who always liked things to be done neatly and quickly, he hated beating about the bush, wasting precious time. Again, the nagging and worrying question: "Where do we go from here?"

Chief Mutare's death would not be announced over the radio. Or, if it did, it would simply be said that "he is missing and has to be found back at a ceremony to be decided on by his colleagues the other chiefs."

And that would happen only after he had been buried.

"But you remember how much trouble he had with the paramount chiefs at home concerning the recognition of his status," Fred put in.

"All those wounds will be healed at or by the succession," Pa Ambrose pointed out. "The administration will be there too to give the occasion the dignity that it deserves and to give his successor legality in the presence of all the chiefs who would be present. The actual burial would be a secret and purely traditional spectacle, there would be no laying in state. You will be allowed to look at the corpse again only because you are the son. The rest of the ritual would be executed by masquerades, nobles and a selection from the Fons. The catching ceremony, the ceremony in which the new chief would be enthroned, is the thing and after the burial it would be decided whether the successor together with his entire cabinet would be chosen in conclave and

144

then presented to the public during the ceremony or they would be assembled and be caught during an open display of traditional manifestations..

It was concluded that the late man would not be kept in the mortuary, he would be taken that same night and kept in a room in his compound. Word would be sent to the village and to the Governor's office.

"That's it?" Fred enquired.

"That's it," he was told.

A larger committee was immediately voted into place for further arrangements. Fred was not a member of any. It was assumed that he would be too disturbed to be involved. But he was to be informed of all resolution and proceedings as work progressed. The burial took place twenty-four hours after the death. He was buried in the night of the next day, traditionally. Seven paramount chiefs attended the burial. No member of the administration was invited, they were to await the catching ceremony which was set for the second Saturday after the burial. Everything had to be done very fast because they were nearing the end of the dry season and did not want affairs to be disrupted by rains which could start pouring down at any time.

It was only in the morning that Beatrice learnt that her arch enemy had died.

"How did he die? What happened?" she enquired with genuine concern. Although she knew that the man detested her especially when he heard that she and Fred had been secretly engaged, and would have killed her if he had his way, she did not wish him dead. She knew that his death would affect her husband a lot and so never prayed for any such thing.

"He went to toilet and there developed a heart attack."

"I saw you drive out in the ambulance," she said, "but I thought it must be some emergency."

"We were going like that to try to revive him, but it proved impossible. You know the intense nature of my father's life, he was a man to suffer from cardiac arrest some day. He allowed too many things to anger him too severely."

He told her what plans had been put in place. But she had one question:

"Fred, be frank with me, did my presence in this house have anything to do with his death? Could the fact that we are engaged and living together have angered him to the extent that it triggered off some violent emotion that produced the heart attack?"

"No," Fred said flatly but insincerely. "How could it? He simply came here to discuss some family matters, and then it happened. Apparently it might have been building up."

It would have been terrible for Fred to tell the truths surrounding the man's death; to mention, for instance, that he was found dead, clasping her slipper in his left hand, which he clung to so steadfastly that for a while it looked like he would be buried with it. Fred did not hate her so much as to drive her mad by telling her such things.

She did not press the issue, but she continued to feel pangs of guilt because when she escaped into the room at the old man's approach, she could overhear the old man making references to her as he shouted angrily.

Fred sent word to Raymond, one of his few confidants, to whom he told the whole truth about what had happened. He told Raymond what they had been talking about and how at a critical moment of their discussion the man rose and never came back alive. Both of them knew that the old man disapproved of their engagement with all his soul, but they had hoped that with time he would be convinced to pardon, live with it and forget about them completely. But the old man seemed most unforgiving on the matter.

That aside, what seemed to preoccupy Raymond's thoughts was not the fact that the old man had died, but his manner of dying. He told his friend very sincerely and very

146

gravely: "I don't know how it is with you people, but with us the Belakossis, death by suicide is considered an abomination of the first order. The corpse is never touched by any ordinary mortal. If the man died by hanging, a special class of men belonging to a secret society dug a hole directly under the hanging man and then cut the rope so that it fell inside. The hole was then filled with earth again and then an injunction placed on that piece of land. His body was never touched."

"What if he hanged himself in his house?"

"The consequences are the same. A pit is dug on the floor beneath him, he is cut and thrown inside and the Fon places an injunction, nobody ever lives there again."

"But if it is not a case of hanging?"

"If it is proved that he killed himself even by taking an overdose of drugs, his compound is sealed. The nature of his death is announced several times. He is not mourned for in the traditional way, and then his compound is sealed.."

"Until?"

"Forever. And whatever title the man might have had before his death did not matter. As I said, he could not be mourned for, at least not in public and anybody seen showing any emotion at his death pays a very heavy fine "

Fred shook his head and reflected. He felt nervous as never before and he could not hide it.

"So what do you suggest that I should have done?" he asked his friend with trembling lips.

"I am not suggesting anything. I was merely telling you what obtains in our own tribe. Customs differ, yours may be very different, I don't know. Did you try to verify that from those old people? Or simply thought death is death?"

"I verified nothing," Fred said almost to himself. He did not tell Raymond that most tribal customs are the same and that certainly in the Bego-Ntsen custom suicide was equally regarded as an abomination, although he did not know the details. He did not tell Raymond that the reason he feared revealing the real truth surrounding the man's death was because of the effect he thought such a revelation was sure to have on Beatrice. He did not tell Raymond that in anybody's mind, to say that his father killed himself in his house because he refused to send away Beatrice was tantamount to murder. People would say he had killed his father, or that his wife had killed her father in-law.

"At any rate," he said, trying to rise above the confusion into which his mind had been thrown by what his friend had just said, "I have already told them that it is a case of cardiac arrest."

"Let's leave it at that. I did not even mean that you change what you have said. I grew up very close to the tradition of our people and whenever a situation arises in which aspects of culture are involved, I become very vocal. I just felt obliged to tell you the cultural implications for our people, if that happened in our tribe. Let's just hope that tradition does not pin us somewhere down the line."

Fred tried to tell himself that it simply did not matter, but the thought of it continued to bother him.

"Are you that superstitious, Ray?" he asked his friend, trying to mask his own fears and suspicion.

"I am not superstitious in the generally understood meaning of the word. But that is quite a different thing from believing or not believing in tradition. For instance, I do not see a thunderbolt striking anybody dead just because you concealed the truth about your father's suicide."

"Let's say in your tribe, such a thing as I have just done happens, what can be the consequences?"

"Doc, you are pushing me to say things I am not sure of. I cannot tell what the consequences can be because the laws are clear on that, the people know it and have never, within living memory violated it. I cannot, therefore, talk of consequences."

148

"But, let's presume that it finally happens, imagine what the consequences can be," Fred pressed on.

"That I cannot say."

"However, what's done is done, and cannot be undone. Let's get to business," Fred said and proceeded to tell Raymond the programme.

Chapter Sixteen

For the next couple of days Fred and Raymond and the rest of the family did the laborious planning. Raymond and Fred took care of the Government officials, civil servants and friends who were to be invited from the province or even beyond. Pa Ambrose, Mbe Mimba and other co-opted senior members of the tribe worked on the list of the Fons who were to be invited from back home, the different jujus and dance groups and the order of their appearance.

Raymond arranged for six canopies and some music which would provide a background to the ceremony whenever the drums were not playing. It was he who took the programme to the Senior District Officer for final approval. The man made only one modification, or rather cancellation: he said there would be no gun-firing. Quite recently there had been far too many deaths resulting from gun fires at death celebrations. Dane guns were said to have exploded, killing their owners, while others with solidly manufactured guns were said to have slipped during the event, shooting and killing innocent bystanders. This information was received by the tribesmen as a big blow to the event. A catching ceremony without gun-firing, one chief said, was like soup without salt, tasteless. If it were not that the man accepted to be personally present, it would have been concluded that the Government did not approve of the request to hold the ceremony. Raymond was also carrying a sealed letter to the S.D.O. It was a letter from the Traditional Council bearing the name and identity of the person who had been chosen to succeed Chief Mutare 1.

Saturday, exactly ten days after the burial of Chief Mutare, was the day of the big event. To the left of the front yard where Chief Mutare planted yams, everything was pulled down or pulled out and the ground levelled and three big canopies raised and labelled. Under these canopies would sit the Fons, the Sub-chiefs and the nobles or simply the "Beukems." To the right the ground was also levelled and two smaller canopies set up. The S.D.O (short for Senior Divisional Officer) and his entourage which usually included other senior Government officials, were to occupy one, while other V.I.P.s not belonging to the Government sector were to occupy the other, both of which were appropriately labelled. In the centre was another canopy where the players of the various dance groups would sit.

The ceremony was to begin at ten o'clock with the arrival or appearance of the Fons and Paramount Chiefs, most of whom had come the day before and were spending the night in the neighbourhood so as to be in time for the event. Everything and everybody, the musicians, the choir groups, the drummers, the dance groups, was supposed to be set so that as soon as the S.D.O. arrived at 11 they would kick off. When all was set, the S.D.O. was sent for. It was to be a day of misfortunes and it began rather ridiculously, confusedly. As soon as the S.D.O. appeared at the gate, everybody rose for the National Anthem. To everybody's embarrassment, two different groups rose to sing.

The point was that the Lemoh-Begoa Family Choir had just completed learning how to sing the National Anthem in their own dialect, a feat which they were anxious to display. This was the first real opportunity for them to display their competence and they were not ready to let it slip. But, down to the last minute, they had not agreed with the Primary School Band which was being led by the headmaster, a personal friend of the late chief, who thought that was the last opportunity for him to honour his late friend. A compromise arrangement was arrived at whereby the Primary School Band would play the anthem and them make way for the choir to sing it in the vernacular. It was for this reason that the two groups moved to the centre of the arena. Luckily for the choir, and perhaps luckily for the organisers, the band fumbled twice and departed in disgrace. What happened was that at their last practice the previous night, the headmaster, threatening them with a cane had warned:

"I know that there are some of you flutists and even drummers who are still not good enough. But we shall not keep you out. If you know that you are not sure of what you are doing, don't just fold your hands and stand. Flip your fingers as if you are playing the flute. And you the drummers, make as if you are playing the drum, but do not play, those who know should cover the others."

And so when he gave his signal for the National Anthem, his boys, none of whom was sure of his performance, merely pretended to play: the flutists flipped their fingers, but did not blow, each hoping that the other knew better and would cover him up; the drummers held their sticks over the drums and shook them vigorously, each drummer, doubtful of his performance, hoped that his friend who definitely knew better than himself would cover him up. As a result, to the embarrassment of the headmaster, but to the happiness of the Lemoh-Begoa Family Choir, not a sound came out. He gave another signal, again the boys only pretended. Furious, he marched the boys out and away to be trashed. He would say later that his band had been bewitched by the Lemoh-Begoa Family Choir. But, be it as it may, there were silent chuckles as he went out shamefacedly, holding his head down. It was at this juncture that the Lemoh-Begoa Family Choir seized the floor and thrilled everybody by singing the National Anthem to the finish in their dialect.

The S.D.O., dressed in his official uniform of well ironed khaki and adorned with medals and badges and wearing a large hat of office, was led to his seat amidst loud cheers, while Raymond's D.J provided an accompaniment of mourning music in the background. The Lemoh-Begoa Family Choir could not regain its seat as soon as it finished singing because people kept coming up to congratulate them by giving them money. Some gave coins, some gave five hundred francs, some a thousand francs and the really big men gave five or ten thousand francs. When they finally left, the M.C. took the floor and very quickly sketched the programme. He stressed on speed and quickness of action because they did not want the rain to interrupt the activities. There were to be fourteen different dances, corresponding to the fourteen Chiefs who had attended. When each dance was announced, representative dancers of the fourteen different groups would dance together, in order to save time. Each dance group would be led by a small boy or girl holding a placard bearing the name of the Fon or Paramount Chief it represented. Apparently they had all been briefed the previous evening about all this. He read out the names of the various dances and the order in which they were to dance down from the gate into the arena. He told all the dance groups to go out of the gate and only descend when it was their turn to display. He concluded:

"His Excellency the S.D.O. cannot spend all day here with us. So, after the third dance, the Fons and the Paramount Chiefs will present the new Chief, Chief Mutare the Second, to him and the public. Thereafter, he will be free to leave us. And after the fifth dance the sons and daughters of the late Chief would gather in the arena and dance with the masquerades, during which the new Chief's cabinet will be caught."

The first dance was "Nkwé," and even before he finished, the drummers had begun. There were two long drums, two small ones, two sets of xylophones and plantain stem and a large *nteuh* and a much smaller one, which were struck with two short sticks. The men at the long drums beat furiously, joined by the small drums, and then by the *nteuh*. All the musicians wore only loincloths tied round their waists and one could see their muscles flexing and unflexing as they struck their various instruments. Then a dancer charged into the arena, sword in hand, little bells ringing about his feet. He put up a one-man show in front of the drummers: vibrating like a weaver bird in the rainy season, he stood on tiptoes and cut a dance forward and then backward for just about one minute; then he swung himself right round with great alacrity in front of the drummers and halted abruptly, pointing his sword at the drummers. The drums stopped beating with military precision, amidst great cheers. He immediately ran back and led the various groups of the "*Nkwé*" dance into the arena, who also displayed in a circle round the arena. Friends and relatives rushed into the arena to pin coins and notes on the sweaty faces of the dancers and drummers to encourage them and to compensate them for a job well done.

The second dance was the "Lenya," and then came the third, the "Abin," not so much a dance as an ostentatious display of affluence. The dancers were great nobles whose dress showed great wealth and power, very expensive velvet, lace and other articles of clothing which people price very highly. Their dance involved merely opening out the clothes and stretching them out for the public to see and applaud. And the public did.

And then, the climax of the ceremony, the presentation of the new chief! Everybody regretted the fact that there was no gun-firing, ears would have split at that moment. Seven Paramount Chiefs went into the room in the house in which the late Chief's Children were sitting and brought out the new Chief, Fon Mutare the Second. He was Bernard who had taken the new title of Fuotambong Mutare II. He was clad in his late father's traditional outfit: a rather large felt-like brownish fabric with beadwork sewn onto raffia weave supported by a cane frame which was covered with blue, yellow, and black beads set off by red felt-like fabric. Two flaps ran from either side of the cap down to the level of his navel. In the middle of the cap were bead embroideries of small spiders with eyes and bodies outlined with white beads worked over little pieces of wood giving it a sculptured-like quality. Around his neck were three rows of blue beads and on both arms were bracelets of brass cast with two little balls on the inside which rattled with every movement. He was wearing a down-reaching gown of cotton embroidery decorated with red, yellow and white designs of lizards, hearts, double gongs and spears all round from the front to the back.. In his right hand was the staff of office. It had a wooden shaft, a triangular, iron tip with a flat rattle and two rows of twisted bards. A brass wire was coiled around the shaft beneath the socket. On his side hung a large sword in a scabbard. The sword had an iron blade spiked into X-shaped wooden hilt with an overlay of small copper plates. The scabbard was basically of wood covered with something like goat or antelope leather. Cords embroidered with blue and white beads in spear motif on the upper and lower edges. The back was undecorated. A cloth sash holding the sword over the chest and shoulder ran through the handles of cane attached to the sides. The sash had two brass bells with geometric designs on the upper and lower border.

He stepped into the arena and strode majestically behind six masquerades or *Truors,* and between two of the most revered Paramount Chiefs who were also sumptuously dressed. A servant followed behind him holding a large multicoloured umbrella over his head. The rest of the Paramount Chiefs and Fons followed, shouting and shaking their staffs of office in warlike fashion in the air. They marched straight to the S.D.O. and stood in front of him just long enough for him to acknowledge the new Fon's presence with a respectable nod, while the *Truors* put up comical demonstrations that appeared almost meaningless to a stranger, but which were an integral part of the ceremony, and then they marched round the arena amidst great drumming and singing and screaming. Someone was heard blowing the bugle to add spice to the shouting, now that there were no guns. The new Fon was then led to his throne, a large semi-circular high stool with a cloth cover embroidered with blue tubular or cylindrical beads, white, red, light blue, and dark blue beads. The seat was embroidered with cowries with serpents framed by a beaded band with spear motif and a band of cowries. The wall behind it was covered with traditional blue cloth. The skin of a tiger hung behind him while another lay in front of the throne on which he placed his feet. On either side of the throne was an elephant tusk.

Something has to be said of the *Truors* who led the new Chief to his throne and continued to linger in the arena for a long time, pinning their spears in front of important officials and demanding money. Back home in the village where it originated and from where it had been transported to K-Town by the visiting Paramount Chiefs, it was a secret society, the highest in the hierarchy of secret societies in the clan. Dressed in "mukutas" or jute bags which covered their faces and with a green leaf from a sacred grove on the top of each one's head, they were incarnations of the ancestral spirit. As incarnations of the ancestral spirit the *Truors* were believed to be supernatural, invulnerable and so immortal. Whenever a Chief had some dirty job to carry out, it was in the hands of the *Truors* that he entrusted it. If the truth of Chief Mutare had been made known, it was the *Truors* who would have buried him, and it would have been the *Truors* to put the injunction in the entrance into the compound where he died. If a Chief proved obnoxious and the people thought of removing him from office, it was the Trours who carried out the act. The *Truors* could even eliminate an individual considered a threat or a danger to the throne. A dreaded society from time immemorial, they had only one irredeemable weakness, it was always begging. It would beg from a man, beg from his wife, beg from a child standing with them and even from a baby on its mother's back. There was an expression in the Bego-Ntsen dialect: to describe somebody as a *Truor's* bag, implying inordinate greed. However, this did not diminish the Truor's importance and respect. The only sign of humanity in the *Truor* was the feet and the hands. It was hard to understand the *Truor* because it spoke only through the nose or simply hissed and made signs. Every Fon had a good number of them to protect his palace and guide him in his kingly duties. In the days gone by *Truors* carried only walking sticks with which they blocked the way of their victims until they had been given something or as much as they wanted. But in recent years *Truors* carried spears to frighten people and make them give more than they would have liked to do. And so the *Truors* lingered about, hissing, barking through the nose, begging or rather extorting money from visitors while the drums beat and the Fons fanned the new Chief to his seat.

The choice of brother Bernard as the new chief was very appropriate in some way. Although any of his junior brothers could have been selected, anybody else would have had to work very hard to know what Bernard already knew just from hanging around his late father. He was the first son by his father's second wife who had been a thorn in Chief Mutare's flesh. She was always complaining that her husband had spent all his money on Fred whom he had sent to England while neglecting any other son. It was of no consequence to her that her son was so dull that he had not even made it through the First School.

"It is easier to bring England to this house than to send Bernard to England," Chief Mutare would say. "You think that is how they go to England, when you cannot even write your name?"

But Bernard had one redeeming feature which his father appreciated very much, he was always with him. When the old man suddenly declared himself Chief and refused to shake hands, and many people laughed at him including even Fred, it was Bernard who stuck by him and carried his bag and mat just as the *nchindas* of other Chiefs did. Because he was always with the old man, he got to know the extent of the man's assets, where receipts of vital documents were to be found, and where witnesses to a certain deal lived. To this extent, therefore, it was appropriate that he had been chosen, especially as Fred had always counted himself out.

But, viewed from another angle, the choice was unfortunate. It was not enough to know the limits of farms or where vital documents were to be found. A Chief needed to be very smart because ruling over people was a complicated affair. It required diplomacy or forcefulness if the situation required that. All these qualities Chief Mutare had in abundance and that was why he was able to work his way from an ordinary family head to a revered Chieftain, a Second Class Chief, a Gazetted Chief. In this his successor was dismally lacking. He was always willing to obey, but he lacked initiative, was indolent and tactless and was sure to bring the throne to shame. He was sure to lose the respect of the other Fons before long. But for the moment, his choice had eased the tensions within the family and left the mother bubbling with pride that she was the mother of the new Chief, something that was envied by all the women in the clan.

As soon as he sat down five stools were brought and placed beside him, two on one side and three on the other. These were the seats which members of his new cabinet were to occupy. Everybody who knew the tradition well knew the various personalities who were to be caught, and in what order. First to be caught was to be the "Mafuo." Although literally it means the mother of the chief, the "Mafuo" was supposed to be of the same rank with the new chief, except for the fact that she was a woman, and a woman could not be chief. Being a "Mafuo" implied that the late chief had a lot of respect for the woman and would have chosen her as his successor if she were a man. It was a very high and respectable rank in the hierarchy of the Fondom. The second person to be caught was the "Ankwetta." This too was a title reserved for a woman. Again, second to the "Mafuo" in the late chief's estimation, the "Ankwetta" could very easily have occupied the chair of rule as successor, if only she were a male.

The third to be caught was the "Mmè-bafuo," or "Mother of the Chief." This office also belonged to a woman and was equivalent to that of a sub-chief. She was the child whose presence reminded the palace and the clan at large of the mother of the late chief. The fourth to be caught was the "Nkwetta." This time it was a male office, and it was given to somebody who could also have been chief but for the fact that only one person could sit on the throne. The fifth to be caught was the "Asa'ah."

The fourth dance, the "nteuh" was staged, it was mainly for men. Four dancers in sleeveless singlettes and wearing loin cloths charged from the lot outside the gate, sword in hand, into the arena where they put up an exciting display, jumping rhythmically to the left, to the right and then they danced in a single file on the same spot. They danced towards the drummers, in front of whom they put up another furious display, ending up with a jump high in the sky and then bowing with their swords pointing to the drummers, the latter suddenly stopped drumming. They ran back and led the fourteen dance groups of that particular dance into the arena and, as they danced, masquerades went round seizing the late chief's children one after the other until the cabinet was complete. It was during this dance that tragedy struck and turned what would have been a memorable day into a day of sadness.

The S.D.O. who had stressed at the beginning of the event that he would want to leave as soon as possible to attend to other state duties was still sitting there, enjoying every bit of the show, the variety of dances and masks, nodding and clapping, even after the fourth dance. Halfway through the fifth dance, the "Nteuh," it began to drizzle. This, however, did not deter the *Truor* masquerades from doing their job. They strode majestically through the rain as if it were sunshine, spears in hand. As the dancers danced out to permit the next dance to come down into the arena, the six *Truor* masquerades who had led the new Fon into the arena, and who had caught the members of his cabinet continued to dance round, brandishing their spears. They would charge towards a group of onlookers or Fons or nobles and make a show of throwing their spears at them, catch the spears in the left hands, turn their backs and then dance to another group where they did the same. The drizzle continued, and real heavy drops could be heard on the canopies. The *Truor* masquerades danced on as the wrenching beat of the drums rose higher and higher and crowds shouted and screamed. Finally, they were facing the S.D.O. who sat nodding as they brandished their spears at him in one last bid. Suddenly they broke into a frenzied dance moving backwards until they were about ten metres from the S.D.O.'s canopy, and then they charged forward in warlike fashion, lifted their spears and threatened to shoot forward as they had done in the other places. By now the rain was actually pouring and the S.D.O. hoped to leave any minute. By some unfortunate accident, perhaps as a result of the rain that had made the handle of the spear slippery, as they threw their hands forward, the spear of one of the *Truor* masquerades actually left his hand and plunged into the S.D.O.'s chest, exactly, Fred would say later to Raymond, the way Chief Mutare had plunged his dagger into his heart.

Pandemonium broke out as the man fell over while blood flowed from the wound. Considering it a planned act, his orderly immediately drew his revolver and shot and killed the *Truor* masquerade who had come and was standing near the dying man, deep in remorse, trying to see the extent of the accident. A second shot wounded another masquerade behind his neck, throwing him to the ground. The Legion Commander who had come as a member of the S.D.O.'s entourage ordered the two Gendarmes with him to round up all the *Truor* masquerades. Instead the men shot and killed another. The men then charged into the palace, beating up anybody in their way, but the charge was useless because the three remaining masquerades who were supposed to be ancestral spirits had quickly changed into their normal clothes so that they were not easily detectable.

At the sound of the gunshot even people who would have liked to lend a helping hand to the wounded man, fled for their lives. The Fons and Paramount Chiefs whose dignity and high positions prevented them from fleeing like infants, also took flight when they saw the Truor masquerades tumble in the hail of bullets. It was unheard-of that a masquerade would be shot at, that he would be made to weep like a mortal. The entire scene was viewed as a slap in the face of the tradition.

The spear was not removed because it seemed to cause the wounded man more pain. The handle was broken to permit him to be carried into the army Land Rover which drove immediately to the Military Hospital, accompanied by Fred and Raymond.

Within a few minutes, the palace ground was filled with soldiers and policemen in combat uniform. This was in response to the Legion Commander's message to headquarters. The spectacle that ensued exceeded in brutality all the crimes of the military and police which the people had ever known. Men, women, children who were found were raped, beaten up, maimed, and even killed. Anybody in traditional outfit, indistinguishable from a Truor masquerade, was marked for capture, torture and death. With the military which was always anxious to exploit disorder to personal advantage, the palace itself was ransacked, the elephant tusks, the tiger skins, the traditional blue cloth, cowried stools and bronze swords and other precious items which the late Chief had spent his whole life collecting, and which had adorned his palace, were confiscated. In all, eleven people died, including three Truor masquerades who to the shocked amazement of everybody, turned out not to be supernatural beings, reincarnations of the ancestral spirits, but ordinary mortals: Marcus Siawey, a bricklayer in the neighbourhood, Aaron Jungi, the chief whip of the Family meeting and Tobias Anu, a Primary School teacher. A contingent of soldiers and policemen was stationed in the palace and a ban placed on all traditional manifestations in the palace or anywhere else in the South West Province.

To justify their brutality, the death of the S.D.O. was given an entirely different interpretation: it was said that he was murdered because he had often decided land disputes against the Lemoh-Begoa people in general and Chief Mutare in particular. Some said that he had been killed because he banned gunfire. Five of the elderly Paramount Chiefs who had come down from the village and who could not escape like the younger ones were rounded up, derobed, beaten and taken to the Gendarmerie where they were tortured almost to the point of death. Fon Mutare II managed to flee but he was eventually captured and taken to the Gendarmerie where he received his own share of the torture.

Fred was not permitted to be part of the team that operated on the S.D.O. who was still breathing and writhing when they arrived the army hospital. He did not go away. He handed to one of the doctors his business card bearing all his qualifications.

"Just in case you may need my help, I am outside." And then he retreated to sit on the bench outside with Raymond. He was anxious to know the precise fate of the S.D.O. After about an hour, one of the doctors came out and invited him and they hurried back in. He was given a mask and then an apron and gloves and he soon became an important part of the team which worked on the S.D.O. The spear was carefully removed and they were able to see the exact extent of the damage. It had grazed the left common carotid artery, but not fatally. The wound was patched and the man's chest sewed up and while he recovered from the anaesthesia, Fred rejoined Raymond on the bench.

"He will make it," he told Raymond. "The shot was not fatal, though it could have been. He should come through in an hour." Then the two men sat pensively, saying nothing to each other for a very long time. As if rising from deep sleep, Fred turned to his friend:

"Ray, the S.D.O.'s plight aside, are you by any chance thinking about what I am thinking?"

"Raymond's lips pulled apart in a mirthless smile and then he asked:

"What are you thinking of, doc? The traditional thing?"

"Yes," Fred nodded grimly. "Is that what you are thinking?"

"It's terrible."

"Tell me, Ray, were you thinking about what we discussed the other day concerning the consequences of the fact that I hid the true circumstances of my father's death?"

"I was," Raymond said and then added, "as I said the other day, we should never underestimate what could happen if traditional custom is violated."

"This is terrible, Ray. As soon as the S.D.O. collapsed and panic broke, that was the first thought that came to my mind. I feel terribly guilty and afraid. Really afraid."

Then the silence fell again until a doctor came out and took Fred in. The S.D.O. had regained consciousness. They led him into a private room for V.I.Ps in the reanimation ward. When he saw Fred he smiled tiredly, turned his face and fell asleep. Reassured that the man wouldn't die, Fred and Raymond drove off and then went home.

Although the man had survived, the news all over the city was that he had been killed instantly. That very night Fred eased the tension somewhat by telling the soldiers and policemen in the palace that he was alive. He also informed Mbe Mimba and Pa Ambrose about it and several other people. He also went to the radio and informed some journalists. Thus, before morning, it was widely known that the S.D.O. was alive and in a critical but steady condition, in the military hospital. But he could not be visited by anybody not of his immediate family.

When he returned home he found Beatrice reading the Psalms, Psalm twenty-three, to be more exact. She received him in gloomy silence. She had followed much of what happened over the radio. For some reason she had vehemently refused to attend the ceremony, and it was a good thing that she refused because, as things turned out, she might very easily have been one of those victims. Apart from the radio, many eyewitnesses gave her a graphic account of what had happened. She did not mention it to anybody but in the deep recesses of her mind, and given the knowledge which she now had about the happenings from the day of the old man's death, she had the odd sensation that her presence in the family was partly responsible for the misfortunes of the day. Had the old man not found her shoe in Fred's parlour on that day he might not have killed himself. There would, therefore, not have been any catching

165

ceremony in which the S.D.O. had been shot, giving rise to so much bloodshed. All the accusing fingers of those who knew the real truth, were pointing to her and with these feelings of guilt she aged overnight, like a flower that had been plucked from the stem and left to wilt in the sunshine.

The day after the death of her father in-law in their home, she had looked for and found her missing slipper when she had responded to a carpenter nailing something on the door of the public toilet in which the man had died. When she asked what had happened to the door, while the carpenter answered that it had been pulled down by force, Blasius, the yard boy only stammered and kept quiet, drawing her immediate suspicion.

While she was still wondering what had happened she noticed bloodstains on her

slipper which had been discarded the previous evening in the wake of the confusion that arose following Chief Mutare's death. When she insisted, and promised to keep it a secret, Blasius told her the truth, that the old man had stabbed himself, and that he had died clinging to her shoe. Right away a rift began to develop between the two. She waited for Fred to tell her the truth, but he wouldn't. He didn't even want to dwell on the topic of the man's death. When in the end she revealed that she had learnt the truth Fred was even more angry, so angry that he could not even tell her that he kept the truth away from her because he did not want her to feel guilty or hurt. Meanwhile, Fred continued to feel miserable at the thought that the stabbing of the S.D.O. and the consequent disruption of the ceremony and the shame it brought on the tribe may not have been an accident after all, that it was just retribution from the ancestors for the act of concealing suicide under the guise of cardiac arrest and misleading the tribe to engage in a public ceremony over the dead man without the appropriate cleansing.

And with these thoughts, he lost touch with all reality. His practice and his research seemed to abruptly come to a dead end. The flame of love for his job and his people seemed extinguished once and for all. Thoughts of the old man's suicide which now filled his mind took on the terror of a murder guilt and he was haunted by his spirit as if to avenge a hideous crime. The death smothered something in him or was it everything? His elan vital was gone and his demise took the form of small talks in canteens, in the club houses and, most of all, amongst family members who had lost a patient or patients at his hands. He was even described somewhere disparagingly as Dr. Mortuary, to suggest that he was in the habit of sending patients to the mortuary.

The bad part was that he was conscious of his declining practice, of the disgrace and shame that trailed him. He piled unopened letters in stacks, along with numerous others he was lucky to open but never finished reading. Sometimes he would gather all those he had only partially read or opened and did not read and stuff them into the wastepaper basket. His dutiful cleaner Elias would discover them, take them all out and file them and leave on the table in his office. He would not reprimand Elias. Perhaps he did not even notice that there was such a document on the table.

The letters frightened him. It was as if he had committed a crime and feared it would be discovered and hated to hear from people who were likely to threaten him with exposure. The letters seemed to annoy him simply because they reminded him, or made him think of what he once was and what he would have been. The letters, on the other hand, addressed themselves to a genius, a man bubbling with enthusiasm, good health and boundless ambition. But they were received by the trembling hands of a burnt out, exasperated, drink-sodden, unkempt doctor whose mere appearance scared patients. The three volunteers refused to believe what they were beholding and considered his

167

strange behaviour as some temporary lapse that would sooner or later disappear and leave the man to carry out his marvellous work. But there did not seem to be any end to it, instead it grew worse and worse.

The three volunteers, even though they were addressed "doctors," were not doctors in the strict sense of the word. They were fourth year students of a seven year course in the medical school whose studies had been interrupted by compulsory military service, at the end of which they had lost the enthusiasm to pursue studies to the end. They were not surgeons, although they could give some advice and even assist during major operations. They were still to learn a lot from working with Fred in the theatre. The two young black doctors were yokels, too filled with the spirit of young graduates to be trusted with delicate operations. With Fred gone berserk, it was as if the linchpin that held everybody and everything in place had gone. Stories spread like cancer cells and patients declaring themselves healed, vamoosed from hospital beds.

The three volunteers would listen to Fred's gibberish with great amusement until it became clear that the legend was losing his mind, that he was gradually losing touch with reality. Female patients who had no idea that anything was wrong with him fled from his consultation room with tales of molestation that left everybody else embarrassed, shocked. Those who were still planning to visit the hospital thought twice and decided to go elsewhere.

The climax of it came one day when a senior civil servant presented with a case of a swollen stomach accompanied with violent pain: during one of his saner moments Fred diagnosed it as a ruptured appendicitis which could prove fatal if not operated upon at once. It was the kind of delicate operation that called for an expert, not a gambler. The theatre was set and all instruments assembled and then he got dressed for the operation as soon as the anaesthetist finished his job. Before every major operation, they usually prayed or meditated for about a minute, no more. But on this fateful day, with three nurses standing at his service round the table, and with one of the volunteers and one of the black doctors looking on, Fred sat down for ten full minutes meditating on God knows what. Then he began the delicate operation. After thirty minutes he reached the inside of the man's stomach and pulled out the intestines and stretched them out until he discovered the ailing portion which he clipped and stitched. At that moment it appeared that he felt slight tiredness in his eyes and nerves, and the nurses noticed that he was performing with far less than his usual confidence and perfection. He was going about it as if he was operating on a corpse, not on a human being under the influence of anaesthesia the effect of which may expire at any time.

Then leaving the man's stomach still open he took a break! In ten minutes the patient revived to find his intestines sprawled on the operating table. The nurses panicked as the patient struggled to climb down from the table. Dr. Frederick Ngenito was nowhere to be found. Another doctor was immediately sought, a further dose of anaesthetic administered and the man's stomach sewed up. But the patient never regained consciousness. Dr. Ngenito was later discovered lecturing in the canteen about his achievements at Edinburgh and the medals of honour he had won, a full glass of gin in his trembling hands. Of late he toyed with the medals as though they were some talisman with powers to restore his sanity.

Everybody was appalled when it was circulated amongst the staff that he had abandoned a patient in a critical stage on the operation table and gone to drink. The story got to the ears of relatives of the dead man who immediately sued the hospital for damages. The case was still pending. The Board of Governors for the hospital met and decided that Dr. Ngenito should be restricted to administrative work in his office, that he must be restrained, if possible by force, from entering the theatre and the wards, that he was not to consult any patients in his office.

"I know what you are all talking about," he would burst into a group of nurses conversing. "You are talking about me, doctor Frederick Ngenito Mutare or doctor Mortuary as you have been calling behind my back. You are wondering what is wrong with me. Even me myself, I have been wondering too." Then he would burst into a long uproarious and meaningless laughter that left everyone embarrassed. Then he would saunter into the canteen. As soon as they saw him coming they would take away the whiskey and any other strong drink from the counter. When he noticed that he began to come with a bottle of whiskey in his pocket which he drank as much as he could and abandoned the rest.

He stopped making his rounds, or rather he was not included amongst the doctors who made the rounds in the mornings and evenings. This was a far cry from the doctor three years ago who was said to have no closing time. At that time he looked at his closing hours with regret because he hated to abandon his patients. He would go from ward to ward, his patients were his best friends, he knew every case and every patient by name and was the last to leave amongst all the workers. And he only left because the patients with whom he was conversing showed signs of falling asleep.

Now things were different. All that dedication, all that vaulting ambition was gone. A new day, if he was lucky to have his wits with him, if he had not taken more than enough whiskey, was like the beginning of a new trial at the foot of a mountain, from which, most disturbing of all, he was not sure to emerge victorious. He groped, consumed with doubt and uncertainties where he had waded with his head held high in confidence, his breast bristling with new-found ideas.

Chapter Seventeen

The Board of Governors spoke to Fred in the morning of Tuesday. After lunch break, as was agreed amongst the members, the President and the Special Adviser invited Beatrice, the woman everybody knew to be his wife. The President of the Board of Governors was the Secretary General in the Governor's office. When he invited Mrs. Ngenito for a talk after they had taken the decision on Dr. Ngenito, the Special Adviser to the Board was with him. The poor woman could not by any stretch of the imagination figure out why she was being summoned to the Secretary General's office. They received her very kindly, courteously inviting her to sit down in an armchair opposite the Secretary General.

"Madam," the President began, "do not be surprised that we have invited you to talk to you. We are of the Board of Governors of the Mutare Hope Rising Clinic."

She breathed in and out nervously, readjusted herself. Hope seemed to flare up in her, causing a pleasant tremor in her fast beating heart.

"I am listening, sir," she said

"It has to do with your husband."

"What about him?"

"Madam, you sound as if you have not noticed anything wrong with him."

"Well, sirs, I know that he has not been himself these last months, but I ascribed it to the fact that he had just lost his father, which disturbed him very much."

The man nodded.

"Madam," he resumed, "we were also inclined to think that the death of his father may have weighed too heavily on him. But it has turned out that he has a different problem, one we cannot diagnose, but one which affects his job so…" the man stopped, held down his head as if to hold back tears. Then he shook his head briskly and said:

"It is painful to think, madam, that the man who has done everything, the man because of whom we are here, should suddenly become incapable of delivering the goods."

"How do you mean, sir?" Beatrice asked. It was only then that she became aware of the spaciousness of the room in which they were sitting, the mahogany panelling of the walls, the mottled Persian carpet on which stood several small tables surrounded by armchairs and sofas, the expensive drapes on the windows and doors.

"Tell her," the President turned towards the Adviser.

"Madam Ngenito, the President has put the tragedy as mildly as he possibly can. Your husband can no longer treat patients. When given the opportunity, he hurts them, he scares them. And as a consequence, the Board of Governors met today and decided that he would be limited to his consultation room, that even there he would not be allowed to consult patients. His actions right now, are undoing the very good work he has done for us and for this country. The hospital is losing patients and clients by the minute, all because of Dr. Ngenito's unfortunate state. We thought it necessary to inform you of our actions because you are the closest person to him and you might want to see what you can do to get him back on track, if that is possible. Failing that, we were even considering sending him to Zero Zero Centre…"

"To what, sir?"

" Zero Zero Centre…"

"But that is an institution for mad people. I was thinking…"

"It is as bad as that, Madam, but we are left with no other alternative. It has taken us a terrible effort to arrive at that decision on such a great man. Although this hospital remains your husband's brainchild, Madam, we cannot allow him to drag it down with him. Everything must be done to keep it alive, to keep it going, even without him. That is the only way open to us. The lives of many families now depend on the existence of this hospital."

As soon as Beatrice got home he sent word to Raymond. When he came he immediately asked her with visible signs of uneasiness:

"Where's my man? Where's Fred?"

"You know he doesn't have any closing time. He has never had it." She paused for some time and then began: "Anyway, Mr. Raymond, have you noticed something unusual in the way your friend carries himself?"

Raymond nodded several times and immediately a sense of guilt came over him because he became aware that he had not discharged his duty well as a friend of the family. It should have been him to put such a question to her, seeing that he spent far more time with Fred than she did. As if reluctantly bringing out of the depths of his mind some weighty and unpleasant thought, he admitted: "It is unfortunate, madam. Very unfortunate. I have noticed that he has not been himself since his father passed away, but I thought it was a temporary crisis. I could not, for once, imagine that it had come to stay, or that it would grow any worse."

"It has grown worse," Beatrice said, "to the extent that the Board of Governors of the hospital has decided to keep him away from patients, from the wards. You can imagine what that will mean to Fred."

Raymond shook his head sadly. "The odd thing about it is that it comes on him in fits, it is not a continuous mode of behaviour, whatever it is. So that you have to know him very well and watch him closely over a long period to notice that there is something the matter. But quite recently the fits have become more and more rapid."

"What do we do, Mr. Raymond? The Board even considered sending over to Zero Zero Centre."

"We may end up agreeing with them, madam, because we have no choice." Zero Zero Centre was the last resort for unmanageable mental cases, a place from which few patients ever graduated or ever survived for more than a few years. Patients admitted into Zero Zero Centre were bad cases, which could only get worse while there because there were no real experts there to help the deranged patients. He did not tell Beatrice that he himself had thought of that. He did not tell her how often the three volunteers had talked to him about his friend's terrible decline. He did not tell her that he thought it was his violation of the tradition that had caught up with him. He could not mention Chief Mutare's death without implicating her, and this he did not want to do. She had enough problems already, he thought.

Fred returned home to find the two of them together. Raymond's presence alone with his wife did not disturb him, even in that confused state. He trusted Raymond with his life, and knew that he would never betray him. Raymond was happy that he met them because it would then be possible, now that his wife had been alerted, to find a solution together. He did not behave as if there was anything wrong with him. He ate his supper calmly, asked for a glass of wine which Beatrice reluctantly gave, cleaned his mouth with the table napkin and then went to join them in the sitting room. Beatrice had accompanied him to the table but had not said anything to him. She sat back looking for clues of any absurd behaviour.

"How was the day, doc?"

It was as if he had opened a can of worms: Fred instantly turned stammerer; he said something in his throat, but because he was stuttering, nobody understood a word of it.

Then, distractedly, and holding his convulsively quivering face in his hands he said: "Hard to tell which way the world is going. Man is born free but everywhere he is in chains. My whole kingdom, which was the whole wide world, shrunk to a few metres. What a piece of mess is man."

"Fred," Beatrice called as if waking him from deep sleep. "Your friend asked you how your day at work was. How was it?"

She was staring him in the face. He seemed to be terribly frightened by some unfathomable thought and replied at random. She noticed how, from time to time, he cast an unhappy glance at Raymond, how he fidgeted in his armchair at every word that she uttered. Something unknown was obviously bothering him.

"Some blokes came around and spat a lot of bullshit. Anyway, I take it for what it is. I'll just stick in there until, until. Ray," he stopped in the middle of a sentence and turned to his friend. "I think something is not right with me."

"I believe you."

"You believe me, you son of a gun? You notice such a thing and you do not tell me?"

"I was waiting to tell you. In fact, I came to tell you that." He threw a quick glance at Beatrice. She was watching her husband in stark consternation, not a muscle moved on her thin, petrified face. Once in a while she would clap her hands in wonder but without changing her tense and concentrated expression. She had supported her head in her right hand for a very long time, until she felt tired. Now she was supporting her waist.

"Some power has gone out of me," Fred confessed, a desperate sense of defeat pressing on him, a raging sense of hopelessness, of helplessness. "It is as if something that I have done has offended my creator very much and he wants to punish me for it. But what exactly it is, I do not know."

He thought for a while and then asked his friend:

"Raymond, do you think it could be the error I made concerning my father's death?"

"It could very well be," Raymond said noncommittally.

"What a price to pay for one small error. How can we circumvent that, Ray, tell me. I am indeed lost."

Even before Raymond answered he said:

"I would want to regroup. To be left alone to think myself out of this hole in which I find myself. First thing, Beatrice, you will go back to your parents"

"What for, Fred?"

"I just want to see how differently things would be if I am left completely alone."

"If that would help you retrace your steps, Fred, I would go. I really love you, you know. I hate to see you look so confused, so desperate. But something disturbs me, leaves me totally confused too."

"What?" Fred barked.

"Sending me back to my parents at this moment, will seem to everybody else like a divorce. There is no doubt in my mind that we were eventually going to marry in court or in church. But right now I have nothing to show for either. And the baby will come any moment. We haven't made any preparations. We set the date for the court marriage which all these unfortunate events came and shattered."

"Ray, take charge. We go to court on Friday and she leaves on Saturday. I am anxious to try something to see if I can find my bearings again."

"As the court pleases," Raymond said. And then he looked at Beatrice again. "You look so different," he pointed out.

"When women are pregnant, they change. They do not look the same. Or what do you mean Mr. Raymond?"

Raymond had been awe-struck by the sunken nature of her cheeks which were developing wrinkles by the hour. Her staring eyes, encircled by dark unhealthy rings, looked inflamed and red, either from sleeplessness or from recent tears. Her lips, gathering in sorrowful lines, with difficulty concealed some inner mental suffering. These were the changes in her face which he noticed when he said she looked different.

"I must leave you now," he announced. "Something to eight."

Beatrice saw him off to his car and then returned to meet Fred still holding his head in his hands and staring at the floor. When she touched him he jerked his head, smiled tiredly and said: "My father just won't let me go. I see him everywhere, staring at me, threatening to come back and kill himself again, in my house."

Beatrice stood in front of him, speechless, her eyes popping in fear. A burning, unbearable pain pierced her brain and her heart as well. She looked utterly helpless.

The court wedding effective took place on Friday morning at the council office. The Mayor had apparently been hinted that Fred was not in a very good frame of mind and so should be interrogated as briefly as possible. The event was very brief but in the end they were issued two copies of the marriage certificates, one for Beatrice and one for Fred. The following day, Beatrice left for her parents' place. She told them that her husband and herself had agreed that she should be with them until she had had her baby.

On Saturday as soon as Beatrice left for her parents' place, Fred sent for Raymond.

"Let's see how things will work out now that Beatrice has gone," he said.

"Was she the cause of your problems?" Raymond asked.

"That's the way I have been forced to look at it."

"Forced, doc? Beatrice is such a harmless creature."

"But my father's spirits would not let me see her as otherwise. Everywhere I go, they are behind me, urging me to send her away, back to her parents. I see them everywhere, in everything that I do. Once, while I was operating on a patient with a ruptured appendix, I suddenly saw my father's image inside the man, in the intestines I was holding. I threw the damn thing on the table and left. I heard later that the poor man died. My father's spirits pursue me for two reasons: first, they want Beatrice out of my house, secondly they say I killed him. Just look at such a thing."

"Do you believe in spirits, doc? I remember you asking me about superstition the other time."

"It is not a question of believing or not believing in them. This is not a figment of my imagination, it is no hallucination. They are for real, I see them every day. And whenever they say a word to me, my day is ruined."

"We may have to try traditional medicine, doc. There are medicine men who can make it impossible for you ever to see them. I swear, doc, we have to give them a chance."

Fred shrugged. Before Raymond left Fred told him to come and pick him up the following morning so that they could go to church. Raymond came and they went. It was almost as if nothing had ever happened to him to make anybody worried. That afternoon he asked Raymond to take him to Mr. Ebenezar Ebong, the Secretary General at the Governor's office, the President of the Board of Governors. He addressed the man in a manner that left him guilty of the decision they had taken. He told him:

"Mr. President, what has happened to me is terribly regrettable especially as it is happening in a hospital environment where we are supposed to minister onto minds diseased. In the hospital, particularly here when I was in control, we did everything to treat the patient, we do not dump them, even when we know the case is hopeless. I presented with a case of what is usually described in intellectual circles as brain fag, short for brain fatigue. It happens to people like me who bury themselves in research every minute that they are not in the wards. Manifestations of brain fag are systematic loss of touch with reality and, within that frame of loss of touch with reality, so many things can go wrong. But the solution is not to dump the individual, it is to bear with him for as long as it lasts, until he finds his bearing again as I have done."

Mr. Ebenezar Ebong looked first at Raymond whom they had invited and discussed Fred's problem together, and then at Fred. He studied his face and listened to his voice, it was as if he was listening to a replay of his once great self. And with that he began to sense guilt welling up in his mind. He found the accusation justified in spite of the strange and uncanny circumstances under which they hurt him, and found it necessary to apologise. In spite of himself, the man smiled and told him:

"Dr. Ngenito, I am so very pleased to hear you talk like your former self. I honestly wish some other members of the Board were in here with me listening to you. We are no medical men, doctor, we are simple administrators who were called upon to keep watch over the running of the hospital and to raise an alarm if we noticed anything out of the ordinary. Doctor Ngenito, you know that you are not just a worker at the hospital, you are the hospital. If we took the decision that we took, doctor, it was simply because we could not do otherwise and, in our own naïve way, we thought it was best for the hospital. I now regret our actions and wish to render the apologies of the entire Board to you and your family for any embarrassment it may have caused you people. Dr. Ngenito, without even bothering to sound the views of the others, I would suggest that you report back for duty as usual on Monday morning, that is tomorrow morning."

Throughout the entire meeting, Raymond had not said a word. He was still wondering what mysterious thing could have happened to Fred to restore his sanity so suddenly and so completely. He had planted his gaze on Fred while he spoke, and when the Secretary General was speaking he kept nodding in concurrence. They drove back home where he dropped Fred and continued to Barombi Kang.

That same night the Secretary General was so happy with Fred's restoration that in under one hour he informed all the members of the Board. They hovered around the hospital on Monday just to monitor Fred's movements. There was nothing reprehensible in his behaviour, not only that day but throughout the week. During that time, he had no visitations from his father's spirits. All arrangements which Raymond had considered going into to find a medicine man who could block Fred's mind from seeing the spirits were cancelled because he did not complain again. On Saturday the following week, two weeks after she returned to her parents, Beatrice was admitted at the maternity of the hospital and she had her baby the very night. It was a baby boy.

The following morning, Fred sent for Raymond to whom he told what happened to him the previous night:

"My father's spirits appeared to me..."

"Again?"

"Yes, again Ray."

"What did they say this time?"

"That I should not visit Beatrice in the hospital, that I should not see the baby."

"That is madness, I tell you. How can anybody, whether spirit or stone, tell you not to see your baby? Tell them that you must see your baby."

Fred defied the spirits and went to the maternity where he hugged the baby, kissed the mother and danced round the bed. He named the boy after Beatrice's father, not his own. But as they drove home, his old malady returned. Raymond was forced to pass the night with him and when the unusual behaviour persisted, he sent for Mr. Ebenezar whom Fred almost stabbed. Security guards from the hospital had to be called in to bind his hands and feet. Word was sent round immediately and the Board met again. This time there was no threat, given the extent of violence and destruction he had exhibited. Dr. Ngenito was not even permitted to set foot in the premises of the hospital. Sitting between two security men whom he did everything to overpower, and with the younger doctors, nurses and patients wailing and throwing themselves helplessly about in grief, Dr. Frederick Ngenito was transported in the back of his own Land Rover, to the mental hospital at Zero Zero Centre. Raymond went with them. He had not found time to tell Beatrice how suddenly things had changed. But he knew she would soon learn the truth.

How are the mighty fallen!

The hospital lingered on for a whole decade before it was officially closed down by the Ministry of Health for want of proper or adequate husbandry. Although Raymond informed Beatrice that Fred had bequeathed the hospital to her in its entirety, she refused to have anything to do with it. By that time, the three volunteers had long left, recalled because of reports about the declining status of the hospital due to the absence of its founder. Fred spent just one year at Zero Zero Centre and then passed away one night in his sleep. Beatrice returned to her parents from the maternity. Her father changed the name of the baby to Frederick Ngenito, which was the only way of remembering him.

The End